Moon Princess

A MESSAGE FROM CHICKEN HOUSE

When I was young, I had some fantastic imaginary friends – made-up folks and animals who seemed as real to me as the cat next door. The adventures we had together were awesome too, but not as exciting as Barbara Laban's amazing tale where two cultures' mythical and imaginary creatures combine in an all-action race against time!

BARRY CUNNINGHAM
Publisher
Chicken House

Moon Princess

Barbara Laban

Chicken House

2 PALMER STREET, FROME, SOMERSET BA11 1DS

Barbara Laban: Im Zeichen des Mondfests
© Chicken House Germany, Carlsen Verlag GmbH, Hamburg, 2012
First published in German by CARLSEN Verlag GmbH 2012
Original English translation by Helen Jennings
This version © Chicken House 2016
Illustrations © Kate Rochester 2016

First published in Great Britain in 2016
Chicken House
2 Palmer Street
Frome, Somerset BA11 1DS
United Kingdom
www.doublecluck.com

Cover and interior design by Steve Wells
Cover and interior illustrations by Kate Rochester
Typeset by Dorchester Typesetting Group Ltd
Printed and bound in Great Britain by CPI Group (UK) Ltd,
Croydon CR0 4YY

The paper used in this Chicken House book is made
from wood grown in sustainable forests.

1 3 5 7 9 10 8 6 4 2

British Library Cataloguing in Publication data available.

ISBN 978-1-908435-93-4
eISBN 978-1-910655-37-5

For Stefan and our daughters

上海

1 Shanghai – Over the Sea

Sienna's invisible dog, Rufus, had fallen asleep on her lap.

'Mmm, first class,' the little spaniel murmured contentedly, before sinking his nose into Sienna's legs. The dull roar of the plane's engines had sent him to sleep, his long black floppy ears twitching as he dreamt.

Sienna stroked his fur. She was glad Rufus was with her. Her invisible friend had been by her side for as long as she could remember.

Surprisingly, given he could be a little bad-tempered, Rufus had taken the news of the move from London to Shanghai pretty well.

Sienna had been less happy. 'You can't be serious, Dad. Why do we have to move to China? And why now? What about my school, and our home?'

'I don't have a choice,' he replied. 'If I want to keep my job, I have to go to China.'

They were both silent for a moment, then Dad hugged Sienna tightly. 'I can't stay here,' he finally whispered.

Sienna wanted to cry, but she had held back her tears and breathed out heavily against Dad's T-shirt. *And what if I can't go to China?* she thought. But she hadn't said it out loud. She didn't want to make things even harder for her dad. Even though she was only twelve years old, *she* had learnt to be strong for *him*.

Now her dad was sitting next to her on the plane, working on his laptop. The small light above his seat was on. He took off his glasses briefly and rubbed his eyes. He looked tired and sad. Sienna gazed out of the window into the dark sky, Rufus licking her hand in his sleep. It was one of his little habits.

'Stop it, Rufus, that tickles!' she said with a smile.

Her dad looked across at her, tired and irritable. 'Sienna, we've talked about this. You're going to have to stop this nonsense.'

Rufus growled softly, suddenly awake. *'Nonsense?* Is that all I am? I can go if you want. But who will keep you company then, while your dad works and works and works?'

'Shh, Rufus,' Sienna whispered softly. 'It's hard for him to understand.' Then, more loudly, she said, 'It's fine, Dad. I'll be quiet now.'

'You need some *real* friends,' said her father with a frown. 'You can't keep up this rubbish about an invisible dog. What will people think if you go around talking to yourself? It needs to stop.'

Sienna's dad used to make jokes about his daughter having an invisible friend. But now everything was different. Sienna sighed and closed her eyes. A moment later, she heard her dad tapping away on his keyboard.

Mum had always laughed when Rufus appeared. She couldn't see or hear him, of course; only Sienna knew when her invisible friend was with her. But Sienna would translate the things Rufus said for her mother – well, most of them. She kept some comments to herself, such as, 'Your mum should have her hair cut a little shorter, it would make her look younger!'

'When I was small,' her mum had told her once, 'I had an invisible friend called Minka. She was a beautiful white cat. Only I could see her, just like only you can see Rufus. She wore a blue collar with a sparkly bell on it. She was very outspoken but she was my best friend. Some-times, first thing in the morning, she would wake me by softly touching my face with her paws.'

Sienna would have liked to find out more about Minka, but Mum didn't speak about her again. It was as if she was ashamed of her invisible friend. But Rufus had been with Sienna for ever, and she hoped he would never disappear from her life.

'Oh, look. Shall we turn this little TV on? There might be a good movie to watch,' came the voice from her lap. 'And let's order a couple of ice creams!' continued Rufus bossily.

Sienna didn't acknowledge him.

'Oh, come on, they're just waiting for you to order something!'

Sienna stared straight ahead. Rufus *knew* she wouldn't want to annoy her father even more!

'OK, well, ignore me then. See how far you get without me in China!'

And with that, Rufus disappeared. Sienna hoped he wouldn't be angry for too long. She never knew where Rufus went when he disappeared, and he was always vague about it when she asked him. She suspected that he could travel anywhere he wanted, never being seen by anyone else. He certainly seemed to know a lot about the world and often talked of distant places and people.

Dad closed his laptop and looked over at her. His face softened. 'You should sleep now, little one. When we land, it'll be early morning in China, and you don't want to miss your first day there.' He put the laptop in his bag and tipped his seat back. 'Goodnight, Sienna. Sweet dreams.'

Sienna wanted to sleep, but she missed the warm, reassuring presence of Rufus on her lap. Resting her head on her dad's shoulder, she closed her eyes. Immediately she had a vision of her mum sitting beside her. She looked across, met Sienna's eyes and smiled.

Sienna opened her eyes, startled. It had felt so real. So real that she wanted to be lying in Mum's arms, touching her long blonde hair, so similar to her own hair. She could no longer hold back the tears . . .

Sienna didn't know how she managed to get from the plane to the taxi. She hadn't fallen asleep until the early morning light was shining through the plane's windows. Before she had closed her eyes, she had just seen the first grey suburbs of the big city. The vast green hills gave way to houses and straight roads. Then the plane flew across the sea beside the city, and Sienna remembered that the words *shang hai* meant 'over the sea' in Chinese.

She only vaguely remembered waiting half-asleep at the baggage claim, then trudging outside, leaning heavily on Dad's arm. In the taxi she immediately fell asleep again, and as she woke once more she felt as if she was still dreaming, even as she looked out of the car window.

It was grey and rainy outside. They turned on to a huge wide street with cars veering from one lane to another. Ancient buses jostled for position between fancy cars. Sienna watched the people at the roadside. Some were on their way to work. They carried briefcases, talked on their mobiles and seemed in a hurry.

But perched on the pavement there were also men smoking cigarettes and drinking from plastic cups. Some of them were lounging on large red-and-white-checked plastic bags. Their clothes looked old and worn. Her dad had told Sienna that the city was full of migrant workers, men who'd moved from the villages to the big cities trying to find work.

Sienna's mum had spoken a lot about Shanghai. She'd told her about the new buildings that went up every day, and she had shown her many pictures of Chinese cities. Now Sienna saw for herself the glittering towers, some of them endlessly stretching up into the sky. Passing cars and pedestrians were reflected in their facades.

The car was now travelling more slowly and took a turning into a narrow street. Suddenly everything looked older. Cables hung down from the walls at the backs of the elegant skyscrapers, and stretched between the tightly packed houses. Rows of small shops lined the streets.

Sienna would have liked to know what was written on the neon advertisements that hung over the shops, though she could recognize numbers, and sometimes an address – her mum had taught her some of the Chinese characters, which Sienna thought were so beautiful and delicate, like tiny paintings.

Their car passed by a small restaurant. Roasted ducks hung from hooks in the windows. In the entrance to the open door sat a boy, perhaps a year or so younger than Sienna. His dark hair was almost shoulder-length, a few strands hanging in his face.

When the car paused briefly, the boy's eyes met Sienna's. He smiled radiantly, as if he had been waiting for her. Sienna returned his smile shyly and lifted her hand to the window in greeting.

'Ah, you're awake, sweetheart,' said Dad, smiling at her and putting his arm around her shoulder. 'We'll soon be at our apartment block. I hope you'll like it. It's where your mum lived when she stayed in Shanghai.'

The car finally stopped outside a tall, modern building and Sienna and her father stepped out of the car. Sienna held on tightly to her dad's hand. The busy road was full of unfamiliar sounds and smells and she felt suddenly overwhelmed by it all. She imagined her mother here, her fair hair blowing in the wind. Mum had liked these new buildings, even though she was an expert on ancient Chinese works of art. Sienna felt comforted. She liked the feeling of following in her mother's footsteps.

Entering the building's lobby, the taxi driver carried their luggage into the lift before returning to his car. Sienna's father then pressed the button to take them to the fifteenth floor.

2 Jia - Home

'Dad, why do we have to live so high up?' asked Sienna as the lift rushed them higher and higher. She was thinking of their old terraced house in London.

'Most people live in tall buildings in this city,' he replied. 'And I'm sure you'll like the view.'

Sienna wasn't so sure. Heights always made her dizzy. Her dad seemed to have conveniently forgotten this!

When they left the lift they turned right down

a corridor and soon came to a large, heavy wooden door. Dad rang the doorbell, and an artificial bird's twitter could be heard. Sienna and Dad looked at each other in surprise, and couldn't help laughing. They heard the sound of keys jangling and the latch lifting, then the door opened and a strange woman appeared in front of them.

Sienna's first thought was that she was very tall for a Chinese woman, as she stood a head higher than Sienna, and everyone always said that Sienna was tall for her age. The woman's skin was white, and she wore a lot of make-up. Instead of normal eyebrows she had two thin lines above her eyes. Her black hair was carefully styled in large curls. She was wearing a tightly fitted yellow dress.

The woman introduced herself in harshly accented English, giving a wide smile that didn't quite reach her eyes: 'My name is Ling,' she said. 'I am your housekeeper, and your new teacher. Welcome. You can call me Ling *laoshi*. It means "teacher Ling". Come in.'

She nodded to Sienna's dad, and Sienna realized they had spoken before. Then Ling called out something in Chinese and two young women hurried forward to help bring in the luggage.

Dad showed Sienna round the flat. It had a large living room with lots of drawings of Chinese letters on the walls. 'That's calligraphy,' Dad said. 'It's considered an art in China.'

In the dining room there was a huge round wooden table that would seat at least twelve people. 'You can invite all your new school friends round for dinner!' Dad said with a wink. An aquarium, containing three large yellow and white koi, stood in the corner of the dining room. There were three bedrooms: one for Sienna, one for Dad and one for Ling, who obviously lived there too. The furnishings were sparse and reminded Sienna of functional hotel rooms she'd stayed in with her parents on holiday.

'Who is Ling?' Sienna whispered to her father, as they looked out of one of the large windows that framed each room in the apartment. 'And why is she living here?'

'Someone has to be here to take care of you, my dear,' Dad explained, lowering his voice. 'I'm going to be working a lot in this new job and Ling is an experienced housekeeper – she also speaks excellent English. She'll look after you and help you to learn the Chinese language.'

Sienna frowned. Her first impressions of 'Teacher Ling' had not been good!

'Actually, I should check in at my new office. Will you be OK here?'

Dad's voice dragged Sienna out of her thoughts. She could see he looked worried. She was a bit nervous about him going, leaving her all alone, but she didn't want to make him feel guilty. Where was Rufus when she needed him? There'd been no sign of her invisible friend for hours!

She swallowed and forced a smile. 'Sure, I'll be fine. I'll start unpacking.'

Dad gave her a soft kiss on the forehead. 'I'll see you tonight. I'll try not to be too late.'

After her father left, Sienna sat down on her new bed. It wasn't very comfortable and there was only one small pillow. She sighed. Back home in London, her old bed was so soft it had been like sleeping in a cloud!

She went over to the window and looked out.

They were so high up she felt quite dizzy. The city was covered with a large blanket of smog, but Sienna could still see tall buildings stretching as far as the horizon. The noise of the city was muffled by thick glass windows, which couldn't be opened.

She began to unpack: a few books, two of her favourite teddies and her clothes. The room still looked a bit bare. The last thing she took out of her bag was a silver-coloured tin box. The metal felt cool in her hands.

Sienna swallowed, then opened the box. She wouldn't read the letters or emails now; she would just look at the photo that was lying at the top of the box. She put it on her bedside table.

It was a photo from their last holiday as a family. Sienna and her mum and dad were standing in front of a roller coaster at an amusement park. Mum and Dad were kneeling beside her, looking up into the camera. Sienna was smiling and squinting into the sunlight. If she looked closely she could see Rufus in one of the cars on the roller coaster, his ears blowing back in the breeze. Only she could see that, of course. And perhaps only she had noticed that although her mum was trying to laugh, her eyes looked sad.

She remembered what had happened on her last birthday . . .

Sienna was lying awake in bed in the early hours of the morning. Rufus lay asleep at her feet, curled up and snoring softly.

At last she heard the longed-for sound: a key turning in the lock of the front door. Mum! She was supposed to have been home two days ago.

Then she heard her dad's voice in the hall.

'So, Kate, you finally decided to come back, then?'

'I'm so sorry, Alan.' Mum sounded tired and drained. 'I had to postpone the return flight. You wouldn't believe how complicated this project is.'

Sienna heard her dad snort sarcastically. 'So complicated that you've forgotten everything else, apparently. That I have a job too. Or that we have a daughter who misses you so much that she's been crying every night.' His voice was getting louder and louder.

'Please be quiet,' whispered Mum. 'I don't want to wake her.'

But Dad didn't stop. 'Well, at least YOU'RE here

now,' he bellowed. 'Because I'VE had enough!' He disappeared into their bedroom.

Mum came into Sienna's room. Seeing that she was awake, she took her gently into her arms. 'Happy birthday,' Mum whispered.

Her tears fell silently on to Sienna's pillow.

The door opened. It was Ling. She hadn't bothered to knock, Sienna noticed.

'Come, eat,' the housekeeper said shortly, and disappeared into the kitchen. Sienna looked quickly around her room and decided to put the tin box under her bed. She'd find a better place for it later.

In the kitchen there were two large plates on the table. On one lay cooked green leaves in a thick clear sauce: on the other, pieces of bone with meat on them.

'Chinese spinach and chicken,' explained Ling, in her heavily accented English. 'You'll be eating with chopsticks here. You know how to do that?'

Sienna nodded; Mum had taught her.

Ling took two blue-and-white porcelain bowls from a cupboard and filled them with rice from a rice cooker. She placed one in front of Sienna and gave her the chopsticks. 'Lai, you may begin.'

Sienna tried to grab the vegetables first with her chopsticks. Thick viscous fluid, like glue, dripped from the huge leaf into her bowl. How was she supposed to get that into her mouth in one go?

She watched as Ling stuffed a large leaf into her orange-painted mouth with the chopsticks. Sienna had never liked spinach at home, but she forced herself to eat two leaves. She watched in fascination as Ling took a chicken bone between her chopsticks and chewed the meat from it.

Ling noticed Sienna staring at her. 'You Western children don't know how to eat real food. What you all like best is eating fast food. The softer the better.'

Sienna was taken aback. There was real hatred in Ling's voice. She quickly looked back down at her bowl, afraid that staring at Ling would make her even more angry.

'Anyway,' continued Ling, 'here you will eat properly. If you do not eat your meat and your vegetables, there'll be nothing but rice. And you must always use the chopsticks. We'll get started with your lessons after we've eaten.'

The rest of the meal continued in silence. Sienna tried to scoop the rice into her mouth with the chopsticks, holding the bowl tightly under her chin as she'd seen Ling do. She didn't touch the chicken bones.

Her first lesson took place in the dining room. 'From now on we will call this room the study room,' said Ling. 'It's only a few weeks until you'll be starting school. You need to spend the time learning the language of your new home.'

Sienna felt like crying. She'd been hoping to explore the city – now it seemed like she was going to be stuck here every day! But at least she did already know a number of Chinese characters.

'Look, this character is called jia.' 家 *'It shows a pig under a roof, which means "home",' Mum had told her.*

'Please can we have a pig under our roof too?' Sienna begged.

Mum laughed. 'An invisible dog, now a pig – how many more pets do you want?'

Mum could not only read and write Chinese but she was also an expert on Chinese art and history. That had been her job. She and Dad had met each other in China when they'd both been working out there.

Ling put some textbooks in front of Sienna, opened one to the first exercise, and handed her a pen. 'Get started,' she said.

Sienna took the pen hesitantly and tried her best to do the work. Each page showed a different Chinese character. Below the character were thirty empty boxes. She had to copy the character over and over again into the empty boxes.

'Teacher Ling' didn't explain anything. Most of the time she was busy working on her fingernails, filing them into sharp points and then painting them bright red. Sometimes her phone would ring and she'd leave Sienna alone in the room while she answered it.

Sienna soon grew bored with this writing exercise!

And so the first few days passed by in Sienna's new home. Dad went to work every morning and didn't get home until Sienna was in bed. Sienna badly wanted to tell her dad how horrible the housekeeper was, but she didn't want to add to his problems. He always looked so tired.

During the day a cook, Lihua, and a cleaning lady, Shufang – the two young women who had helped them with their luggage – were also in the flat. They barely spoke to Sienna, although they often smiled kindly at her when Ling wasn't looking. Ling left the house regularly, always leaving Sienna with work to do. As soon as she was gone, Sienna would stop working and look out of the windows, trying to get a sense of her new city.

Although she hated being stuck in the apartment, she was actually quite content being on her own. In London she had a few school friends, but nobody she had been especially close to. She had been happy to be by herself and had spent hours reading books or playing cards. If she ever felt lonely, she had Rufus for company. Often Sienna and Rufus would tell each other stories: exciting adventures set in distant lands. But all of that had belonged to another time. Mum had still been with them then.

Now everything was different . . . now *Sienna* was in a distant land.

In the country where her mother had disappeared.

男孩

3 Nanhai - The Boy

Exactly four months ago, Sienna's mother had called from China for the last time. Since then there had been no trace of her.

It took Sienna and her dad a while to realize she was gone. First Mum missed her goodnight phone call two days in a row, but that wasn't unusual, because by the time Sienna went to bed in England it was already early morning in China, and Mum worked funny hours. She hadn't replied to Dad's messages either, but that had happened before – sometimes Mum worked in places without phones or internet.

Dad hadn't been worried until he spoke to the receptionist at her hotel, who hadn't seen Sienna's mother in days. Even Mum's employers couldn't help: Mum often didn't report on her projects for weeks so they hadn't heard from her either. Soon Dad was spending all day on the phone. He spoke to the police, the British embassy and the authorities in the province of Henan, where Mum had last been working. But nobody knew where she was. Finally, Dad left Sienna at her aunt's and flew out to China.

When he returned, several weeks later, every-thing was different. He spoke of the search and of the efforts that had been made to find Mum. He looked like he was trying very hard to be calm. The last time she had been seen had been four weeks ago, when she'd left the hotel in the morn-ing. Mum had worked in several temples in the province, so Dad had spoken to people there too. They had seen Mum around, but not for some time. No one had any idea where she could be.

'Sienna, the authorities have called off the search for your mother. They think—'

But Sienna couldn't bear to hear the end of her father's sentence, and she had run to her room, slamming the door hard behind her.

Dad didn't want to talk to Sienna about her mum. Instead he'd sent her for counselling to 'work things through'. It seemed to Sienna though that the counsellor just wanted her to accept that her mother was dead. Even though she couldn't accept this, she agreed they needed to look to the future now. It seemed to be what everyone wanted to hear, and after she told them this, she didn't have to go to any more sessions.

Sienna secretly believed though that her father also thought her mum was still alive. Dad had said they'd moved to China for his work. But perhaps he hoped they'd be able to find Sienna's mum and bring her home.

It was very early in the morning. Sienna could hear the noise from the street even through the soundproof windows.

She hadn't seen Rufus for days. She wasn't *really* worried about him, as he did sometimes disappear for days on end, but she missed him. She hoped he was OK – Sienna didn't like to think of him lost or scared in Shanghai, on his own! But she had a funny feeling he was nearby. She couldn't put it into words: it was just something she felt deep inside her.

She made a decision: if Rufus wouldn't come to her, then she would just have to go out and find him! Pulling on jeans and a hoodie, she crept out of her bedroom.

The flat was silent, apart from the sound of Ling's snores echoing from her room. Sienna quietly opened the heavy front door of the flat. The air conditioning blew ice-cold on her bare feet. In the stairwell it was even colder than in the flat. Where *was* Rufus?

Suddenly the lift rumbled. Sienna gave a start. What would happen if Ling caught her? She'd forbidden Sienna to leave the flat by herself. She shuddered as she imagined Ling pulling her back into the flat with her sharp fingernails. The lift noise stopped; she could hear voices on a different floor.

Trembling, she pressed the button to summon the lift. Soon Sienna was whizzing downwards. The door opened and she stepped out into the entrance hall. With its marble walls and heavy chandeliers it looked like a hotel lobby down here. To Sienna's relief, she couldn't see anyone around. But as she started to creep past the small porter's lodge, she heard a familiar yawn.

Rufus!

Peering into the porter's lodge, Sienna saw her dear friend lounging on a chair. The porter was nowhere to be seen.

'Well, well, who have we here?' cried the dog sarcastically.

'Oh, Rufus, I'm so pleased to see you! Where have you been?' cried Sienna, gathering Rufus in her arms and inhaling his familiar scent. She hugged him tightly. 'Please don't leave me alone any more. Dad's always away and there's this horrible woman in the flat, who's supposed to be taking care of me. She wants me to learn Chinese all day . . .'

Rufus squirmed indignantly in Sienna's arms until she loosened her grip on him. He leapt back on to the chair and stretched. 'Fascinating as all that is, princess, *I* have something to tell *you*. Now, as you know, I am a sensitive soul and I have had terrible jet lag. That means I'm tired during the day and wide awake at night, or something like that. Anyway, during the times I have been awake – not wanting to wake you from *your* deep slumbers – I have been exploring.'

'You've been out in the city?' cried Sienna, envious of her friend's freedom. 'What did you see, where exactly have you been?'

'Well, I have been exploring the neighbour-hood and finding out some things you might find interesting . . .' Rufus paused dramatically and gazed into the distance.

Sienna sighed. There was no hurrying Rufus when he was in this mood. Looking out into the early morning, she saw that it was still dark outside. The rain ran down the glass door in thick drops, and colourful advertising signs were reflected in the puddles in front of the entrance.

'Do you remember the boy?' Rufus continued. 'The boy you saw outside the restaurant, when you were on your way here in the car on that first day?'

Sienna frowned. 'But you weren't in the car with me! How do *you* know who I saw?'

Rufus raised an eyebrow at her. 'There are so many things you don't understand, princess. Just because you do not see me doesn't mean I'm not with you. Or at least nearby. Anyway, I saw the boy *and* I spotted something special about him.'

Sienna turned away from the window. 'What do you mean, "something special"?'

But before Rufus could elaborate, the lift door opened. The figure that stepped into the lobby was wearing a red dressing gown decorated with flowers. Small, brightly coloured tassels hung from the sleeves and hem. There were lilac high-heeled slippers on her feet, and her head was made huge by the many curlers in her hair, sticking up in all directions.

It was Ling. She stormed over to Sienna, looking like an angry monster. 'What do you think you're doing leaving the flat?' she hissed, towering over Sienna and her invisible dog, who had promptly disappeared. Ling pulled Sienna back into the lift. No sooner had the door closed than she said, with a threatening look, 'I make the rules here . . . and I'll show you what happens when you break them.'

Without Rufus, Sienna felt lonelier than ever before. And what had her invisible friend been about to tell Sienna before Ling had arrived . . . ?

***

Ling made good her threat. She removed all possible distractions from the 'study'. The TV, computer, radio, magazines – even the Chinese ones – all the books, and even the two old armchairs that had been shipped over from their living room in England.

'Too comfortable, it gives you an excuse to be lazy!' she hissed in Sienna's ear as Shufang, the cleaner, pulled the chairs into the hallway. The only things that remained were the large dining table with its heavily lacquered chairs, and two wooden painted calligraphies on the walls.

Breakfast with Ling was the worst part of the day. There was rice soup with dry meat, and when Sienna couldn't eat it, thinking longingly of the choice of cereals and toast she would eat back at home in London, Ling would say triumphantly, 'Too good to eat a decent meal, are we? Just wait until your stomach's rumbling.'

Unfortunately, Ling was right – as soon as Sienna was sitting in the study with her text-books, she longed for lunchtime, even if she knew it would just be stringy meat and veg-etables and rice again.

Every day she had to learn new Chinese

characters. How to write them, how to pronounce them, what they meant. As Sienna swotted up on character after character, she felt like her former life in London had been nothing but a dream. Now she had nowhere to go, and no one to talk to.

Rufus visited her only on very rare occasions. Most of the time he was somewhere else, although he never told Sienna any details about exactly where he'd been. And he seemed reluctant to share any more information about the boy in the restaurant, or what he had meant by 'something special'. After a while, Sienna almost forgot about it.

One day, when Sienna knew Rufus was about to disappear again, she asked him where he was going.

'Oh, I'm just out and about,' he said. 'Getting to know the country and its people, seeing what's going on. *You* should get out more often, you know.'

'Very funny!' cried Sienna. 'I'm locked up most of the time, in case you hadn't noticed?'

'Where there's a will, princess, there's a way. It seems to me you actually *prefer* being on your own,' said Rufus, and then he was gone.

Maybe he was right. The longer Sienna stayed in the flat, the more she got used to not going outside. Her dad, who she barely saw these days, had asked Ling to take Sienna out to some places of interest. But Ling had been quick to put a stop to that. 'The little one needs to settle in first,' she'd said. 'It's noisy and dirty outside, and there are criminals lurking everywhere on the streets. There's no reason for her to leave this flat!'

Instead, whenever she wasn't learning characters or practising her Mandarin, Sienna would lie on her bed, looking out of the windows and dreaming of her mum – or reading printouts of her mum's emails, which she kept in the tin box under the bed, always storing them safely away afterwards.

The day after her talk with Rufus though, when her dad was home at a reasonable time, she asked him if she could go out to the shops with Lihua. Although Ling wasn't pleased about it, Dad thought this was a great idea, and now Sienna would be allowed to go with the cook to the market twice a week, and into the little shop at the end of their street.

That night, Sienna couldn't sleep – the half-moon was bright and the city alive with electric light, spilling in through the floor-to-ceiling windows. She flicked on her bedside lamp and pulled out the box. She opened the lid and shook the entire contents on to the sheets. Letters, photos, pressed flowers . . . all the things Mum had sent to her from China fell into her lap. The printed-out emails, which were folded up in the box, were the only things Sienna had to pull out.

She picked up one of the pictures. She hadn't studied it as much as the others because her mum was behind the camera. It showed a brown car from the side, a young Chinese man waving from the driving seat. He was wearing a white shirt, his hair was blowing across his forehead and he had a beaming smile. *Our new driver*, Mum had written in the border. In the back of the car sat a Chinese woman. Only her profile was visible, framed by carefully styled curls of hair.

Sienna froze. It was Ling!

Ling had known her mother!

A terrible chill ran through Sienna's whole

body as she studied the image closely. She tried to be sensible and think clearly. It was a silhouette through the window of a car – it could be anyone. But it certainly *looked* like Ling . . .

She heard footsteps in the hall and froze. The housekeeper would kill her if she found her awake at this hour! She shoved the photos and letters back in the box under the bed, flicked off the light and shut her eyes.

Her bedroom door opened, and Sienna peeked through half-closed eyes, her heart thumping. But it was Dad. He slipped quietly into her room and sat on the chair beside her bed.

Sienna lay with her eyes closed, enjoying her dad being near her. He held her hand gently. Her breathing slowed and, despite all her questions and fears, she began to feel safe and relaxed.

She drifted off to sleep. She knew she reminded her dad of Mum. Was *she* the reason why he worked such long hours, why he was never home?

When she woke up, later, he was gone. But today was the day she was going to leave the flat for the first time! She pulled on her shoes for her trip to the market with Lihua, already relieved to spend an hour or two away from Ling. She studied the photo of the car again before going downstairs, and though she couldn't be certain it was the housekeeper in the back seat, she had a horrible feeling in her stomach. What if Ling *had* known her mother? Could she have had something to do with her disappearance?

Sienna shook the thought away.

As soon as they turned out of their small alley on to the main road she found the street swarming with people and cars. The air was humid and sticky, and she felt rather overwhelmed by the noise and the crowds after the days spent shut away.

The boy Sienna had seen from the taxi window when she first arrived often sat in front of the entrance to the restaurant with the ducks hanging up in the window. He always wore the same jeans, and a T-shirt with a picture of a Chinese temple on the front. He had a kind, gentle face but often stared at Sienna very intently if she came out of the apartment, which made her feel nervous and curious at the same time. Sometimes Sienna thought the boy might be waiting outside the restaurant just to look for her.

But he wasn't outside today. As Lihua stopped at the vegetable stall next door, Sienna peered through the restaurant windows. The boy was wiping up the plastic tables. Sienna thought again about Rufus's words about him being 'something special'. What had he meant? She thought she saw a flicker of fire above the boy's head – a little flash of light. She blinked. Strange. Sunlight reflecting from a passing car, perhaps.

'Come on,' said Lihua in Chinese, patting Sienna's shoulder. 'We've got lots to buy today – not long until the Moon Festival now!'

Sienna would have liked to talk to the boy, but she was afraid Lihua might tell Ling, and that she would stop Sienna's trips outside. Instead, she quietly raised her hand in passing and waved to him as they walked away. He returned the gesture.

Next weekend Dad was at home, working on the computer while Sienna watched TV. He sat down beside her and gave her hair a quick stroke.

'What do you say to the two of us going for something to eat?'

Sienna jumped at the chance to spend some time with her dad. 'Yes, please! Maybe we can go to the restaurant opposite?'

'Really?' her dad asked in surprise. 'The old cookshop? Well, if that's what you want, then at least we won't have to battle through the traffic.'

They put on their shoes and took the lift down. But, to Sienna's disappointment, the boy wasn't sitting outside the restaurant today. An old man with white hair and not many teeth looked up in surprise as the two foreigners came into his restaurant.

Dad tried to exchange a few words with the man, but he couldn't understand the dialect in which he spoke. Sienna knew her father spoke good Mandarin, or Standard Chinese, but the old people in Shanghai communicated almost exclusively in *Shanghai hua* – Shanghainese.

The man pointed to the menu, a few photos on the wall. Sienna and her father ordered fried noodles and sat down on plastic stools as the man disappeared through a saloon door into the kitchen.

'Sienna, there's something I need to tell you,' Dad began hesitantly. 'I know the move hasn't been easy for you, and that I'm working a lot at the moment . . .'

Sienna swallowed and twisted her hair nervously between her fingers.

Her father continued, 'The bank's sending me inland. To Henan. That means I'll be away for a few weeks. Can you manage without me?'

Sienna continued fiddling with her hair. She would have liked to tell her dad how much she needed him – that he *couldn't* go. That he couldn't leave her alone with a bully like Ling. She would've liked to tell him about the photograph too. But she knew he wouldn't listen. Instead, she raised her head and met his eyes defiantly.

'Of all places, do you have to go to *Henan*?'

Dad stiffened for a brief moment. Sienna knew both of them were thinking about her mum. That she had been in Henan when she disappeared.

He swallowed quickly and said, 'Yes, Sienna, I do have to go there. But it's for work – in a different part of the province. It has nothing to do with your mother.'

And what if you simply disappear there too, and I never see you again? Sienna wanted to yell. But she could see tears welling up in Dad's eyes, and he grasped her hand. Before she could stop herself, she blurted out, 'Are you going to look for Mum? Perhaps if you—'

'Please, Sienna. Don't start that again. The police have done everything they can.' Dad was squeezing her hand so tightly now that it hurt.

At that moment the fried noodles arrived. Sienna glanced up, startled, and found herself looking into the face of the boy.

'*Man man chi,*' he said politely, and sat down behind the counter.

Sienna struggled to concentrate on the food, but she could feel that the boy's eyes never left her for a second. He was looking at her as if he'd known her for a long time.

When Dad got up to pay, the old man came out of the kitchen. As Dad handed over the money to the man, Sienna felt the boy appear beside her. He looked afraid as he put a finger to his lips, passing her a small piece of paper that had been folded over many times. Sienna looked at him questioningly, but the boy disappeared into the kitchen and she saw him raise his hand shyly in farewell.

窃贼

4 Qiezei – Thief

A few days after her father had left for his trip, Sienna was lying on her bed, staring at the piece of paper the boy from the restaurant had given her, as she had done every day since she'd received it. The paper was crumpled and looked as if the boy had been carrying it around in his pocket for a long time.

It was a photograph of a small statue. The figure was wearing a long robe, covering its head and back, and stood on the back of a dragon.

Sienna couldn't be sure but she thought it was a woman. Her delicate face betrayed no emotion, and yet Sienna had seen the expression in countless pictures her mum had sent her from research trips in China of statues and other pieces of art. Strangely, the colour reminded Sienna of moonlight, shiny-white and silvery. *Surely she's royalty*, Sienna thought. Wasn't there a story of a moon princess?

'It definitely looks Chinese,' she murmured to herself. She had never been *that* interested in her mum's job. Nevertheless, she had always liked to sit on her mum's lap and look at photos from her mother's trips to China. Mum had tried to get her interested in temples, statues and paintings. She'd even sent photos of artworks she was working on, along with her letters and emails. This always made Sienna feel part of her mother's world, even though she was a long way away.

'Oh, well,' Sienna sighed, and shuffled over to the edge of the bed. She let her head hang down to look underneath, and saw nothing but a few balls of dust. The silver tin containing her mum's letters had gone!

Sienna felt panic rise within her. Her heart raced. She always kept the tin in the same place. Shufang, she knew, had cleaned her room several times. But she didn't seem to bother cleaning under the bed, and even if she had, the tin had always been left untouched.

A thought occurred to Sienna. Could her father have taken the box away with him . . . ? She shook her head. Even though he didn't like Sienna to talk about her mum, he wouldn't take away all of her most precious mementoes, would he? Sienna decided she had to ask him. Even if he was on a business trip hundreds of kilometres away!

She called her dad using her mobile, but no one picked up. Instead, she listened to a recorded message in Chinese. It obviously wasn't possible to leave a message either. She'd try calling on the landline, just in case.

Sienna crept into the hall. Ling didn't allow her to leave her room in the afternoons, but Sienna wasn't sure whether Ling was even at home. Trembling, she lifted the receiver and dialled Dad's number. The same Chinese recording.

She'd send him an email, then. The computer that they had brought over from the UK was kept in the living room, and as there was no sign of Ling, who had forbidden Sienna to use the computer alone, Sienna switched it on and opened the email program.

Dad had written her a message. In it, he said that China was completely different here, how difficult it was to get around, and how much he missed her. Obviously he was having great difficulty phoning, but Ling had kept him informed on how well Sienna was doing and what great progress she was making with her Mandarin.

Sienna grew angry as she read Dad's email. So he'd spoken to Ling on the phone, probably emailed her too – so why hadn't he wanted to talk to *her*, then?

She pounded the keys furiously:

Please call me. My tin box with Mum's letters in it has disappeared. Do you have it? I miss you, Love Sienna. Xxx

She heard a noise at the door. Ling was back! She'd never make it to her room in time. Sienna quickly shut down the computer and hid behind the large armchair next to the window.

As usual, Ling was wearing shoes with sky-high heels. Each one of her footsteps clicked loudly on the hard floor as she walked into the room.

Sienna peered out cautiously from behind the chair, and gasped: her tin box was in Ling's hands!

Ling placed the box on the table, then closed the living-room door. *Probably doesn't want to be disturbed while she's reading*, Sienna thought bitterly. What was Ling up to? Why would she want to read her personal letters or look at her photos? Ling started rifling through the box impatiently, crumpling and folding the precious papers with her sharp painted nails, digging deeper.

Suddenly realization hit Sienna. Was there something in there that Ling didn't want Sienna to see . . . something she'd *already* seen, perhaps? Sienna's legs began to tremble. She was certain now; it *was* Ling in that photo of the car. The housekeeper knew something about her mother, and she was trying to hide the evidence!

Not for the first time, a desperate, hopeful thought rushed into Sienna's head: *Mum might still be alive!*

At that moment, the bird's twitter of the doorbell sounded. Ling sighed irritably, shut away the papers before she'd had a chance to check all the photos and headed into the hall, leaving Sienna's box on the table.

Sienna heard voices, then Ling returned with a large man. He was Chinese, wore a black suit and carried a briefcase. A chunky gold ring shone on his hand, and a gold bracelet dangled around his wrist. He had piercing, bright blue eyes – Sienna had never seen a Chinese person with blue eyes before.

Ling took a calligraphy picture from its mounting on the wall opposite Sienna. There was a safe behind it! Sienna watched as Ling tapped in four figures, and although the house-keeper's back partly obscured her vision, Sienna knew the combination: 0505. The fifth of May, her mother's birthday. It was the only combination Dad had ever used.

Ling opened the door of the safe, and Sienna saw some of Dad's files and Mum's jewellery box, which Ling drew out. She placed it on the table and opened it.

Sienna clenched her fists. First Ling had stolen her letters, and now she had more of Mum's stuff in her hands! Mum didn't wear it much, but she had inherited a lot of precious jewellery from Sienna's grandmother. When Sienna was younger, her mum had let her play with the sparkling necklaces and bracelets, as long as she was careful.

Now she saw Ling holding these things in her greedy fingers and Sienna felt herself grow hot with anger. How dare she!

The man had laid his briefcase on the table next to the jewellery box. He opened it, and Ling whistled softly through her teeth. Sienna tried to see the two of them properly, but the table was in the way. Risking discovery, she peered over the top of the armchair. Her breath caught in her throat.

Ling took a large necklace, heavy with gems, out of the man's briefcase. Sienna recognized it immediately: it had been her grandmother's! She remembered her wearing it on special occasions. But now the man reached into the jewellery box and pulled out *exactly* the same necklace. How was that possible?

Ling and the man were speaking in an unfamiliar dialect that Sienna didn't understand. Finally the man grinned and drew out a large wad of banknotes. Ling put the money in her handbag and laughed. The man now took the necklace from Mum's jewellery box and packed it away. Ling was holding the other necklace in her hand. 'Perfect,' she said in English.

As it dawned on Sienna exactly what was happening – that Ling was stealing her mother's necklace and replacing it with a copy – she forgot her fear and stood up. Ling and the man both turned suddenly in her direction.

'What are you doing here?' Ling asked sharply.

'What am *I* doing here?' cried Sienna indignantly. '*I'm* watching *you* steal from us! You've had Mum's necklace copied and you're stealing the real one. I'm telling Dad right now about this. You won't get away with it!' She had moved out from behind the armchair and was now close to the door.

'And how are you going to tell your dad about it?' Ling asked mockingly. 'Perhaps you're too stupid to notice, but your father is very difficult to reach at the moment. The only person he speaks to is *me*!'

As Ling was talking, the man had started edging towards Sienna. Beads of sweat stood out on his round face and his blue eyes glistened. He was clutching something in his left hand. Sienna glanced down. A knife!

'Dad will be home soon, and then you won't be able to stop me telling him the truth,' Sienna said, keeping her eyes on the knife and trying to stop her voice from trembling.

'We'll cross that bridge when we come to it, as you Westerners say.' Ling laughed loudly and shook her head, her huge curls looking like dangerous snakes.

Sienna heard the key turning in the front door. It was only Lihua, the cook, returning from the shops, but Ling and her accomplice looked round hesitantly anyway and the man lowered the knife.

All at once Sienna knew what she had to do. She grabbed her tin box from the table. Then she made a dash for the front door, which Lihua had left open behind her, several shopping bags waiting on the landing.

Before anyone could stop her, Sienna ran to the stairwell. She had never used the stairs here before, but she could press the lift button on every floor to slow down Ling and the fat man! She held the tin box close to her and raced off downstairs. Thirteen times she pressed the button to stop the lift; that should give her enough of a start.

Panting, she reached the lobby. She pushed at the front door, but it wouldn't open! For an awful moment Sienna thought she was trapped in the lobby, but then she spotted a button on the door. She pressed it quickly and the door swung wide.

Then the lift came down. Ling and the man rushed out of it, just as Sienna disappeared through the glass doors. They ran out on to the street after her.

At that moment Sienna knew she didn't stand a chance. Where could she go? She didn't even know her own neighbourhood here, let alone anywhere else in the city. She had no money with her, she couldn't speak fluent Chinese, and she knew no one. She ran for a few more metres, then stopped, desperately looking around for the best way to go.

'Now I've got you!' she heard Ling shout as she ran towards Sienna. The Chinese man remained standing by the glass door.

Then Sienna felt someone pulling at her hand. It was the boy from the restaurant!

'*Gen wo lai* – come with me,' he said to her, and without a moment's thought she began to run again.

The boy pulled her into the restaurant, through the kitchen and to a rear exit. Ling tried to pursue them, struggling in her high heels. Sienna heard her screeching loudly behind them as she followed the boy through the narrow alleys behind the shops.

When they could no longer see or hear Ling, the boy stopped briefly and pushed his sweat-dampened hair out of his face. '*Wo shi Feng,*' he said. 'My name is Feng.'

'Sienna,' she panted.

He smiled and together they started running again.

朋友

5 Pengyou - Friend

'*Lai* – come quickly!' Feng called as he pulled Sienna through small, narrow alleys. Her shoulders almost touched the walls to her left and right. They pushed past bicycles and jumped over empty cardboard boxes and bins.

Sienna clutched Feng's hand and tried to keep up with him. Even though she was scared, she felt relieved to be out of the apartment and away from Ling! She realized that they were now in one of Shanghai's old neighbourhoods with *long-tang* houses – a maze of interconnected alleys. Dad had told her about these places. Here stood small one-storey houses, built from red brick and with gabled roofs. Children played in the sparsely cemented streets and alleys.

Sienna was relieved when Feng stopped running a few minutes later and pushed her through a tiny, unlocked door and into one of the houses.

'W-where are we?' managed Sienna, out of breath.

Feng replied in soft, hesitant English. 'This is where I live. You are safe here.'

Sienna looked around the small, damp, empty house. It didn't look as if *anyone* lived here. There was no furniture, just a pile of neatly folded blankets on the floor and a rusty stove in the corner, with one or two pans beside it. The windows were half boarded up, a few planks removed and resting against the sill. The house had clearly been abandoned and shut away. She glanced at Feng, who reddened.

'I live here for now,' he added quietly.

Suddenly she heard a familiar voice. 'What

are we doing here? This part of the city is very dirty and smells distinctly unpleasant!'

'Rufus!' cried Sienna. 'I'm so glad you're here!'

'I wish I could say the same,' snapped the little spaniel, sitting crossly on the floor and licking his right paw.

Feng coughed. 'Who are you speaking to?' he asked with a confused look on his kind face.

Rufus gave a sarcastic laugh. Sienna frowned at him and then turned to Feng. Now was the time to see if all her hard work studying had paid off!

'It's hard to explain,' she began. 'You see . . . I have a friend – a *pengyou*. He's a dog – a *xiao gou* – that only I can see. He's invisible, *yinxing de*. His name is Rufus.' She pointed to where Rufus sat.

Feng stared hard but then shook his head and turned away, obviously unsettled.

'I see *your* new friend is still a way away from recognizing *other* friends,' said Rufus cryptically, looking up from his paw cleaning.

'What do you mean?' asked Sienna. Then she remembered that Rufus has said there was something special about this boy. 'And now you've decided to reappear, you must tell me now what you meant about Feng being "special"?'

'Oh, all will be revealed in good time,' said her friend, yawning loudly as if he were already bored of the conversation. 'Let me just say that you are not the only human to have an invisible friend. Although *you* are lucky enough to have me here with you, others have a more fluid relationship with their companions.'

Sienna turned back to Feng, who was now making a pot of herbal tea on the stove. She wondered if Feng *did* have an invisible friend. If so, perhaps he would tell her about it in his own time. They had only just met each other, after all.

As the new friends sipped their tea, Sienna was lost in her own thoughts. Where should she go? Was Ling looking for her? What were Ling and the horrible man planning on doing with her mum's jewellery? And how had Ling known Mum? She could feel her head spinning, and then she realized Feng was watching her attentively, smiling.

'What is it? What are you smiling at?' she asked, frowning. She didn't find anything amusing about their situation!

'You look very much like your mother,' Feng said softly.

Sienna froze. The colour drained from her face, and her hands began to tremble. Why – how – did this boy know her mother? Leaning forward, she spoke in a voice that didn't sound like her own. 'My mother is missing – *shizong de*. She's been gone for four months. Do you know where she is?'

Feng sat on the chair, deep in thought, looking at his hands. At last, he shook his head.

'But how do you even know my mum?' Sienna asked.

'I come from the city of Pingdingshan in Henan Province,' Feng replied hesitantly. 'I worked in the Fragrant Mountain Temple in the city with Gege.'

'Does that mean older brother?' asked Sienna, who had heard the word 'Gege' before.

'Yes, he is actually called Dewu, but I just call him Gege. We were selling drinks and things. That's where I learnt to speak English.' He paused. 'Your mother came to the temple for her research. She was very friendly. She asked Gege and I many questions about the temple. She found the statue there – the one in the picture I gave you. That's what she was studying when she disappeared.'

'The moon princess?' Sienna asked, but Feng just looked at her blankly.

'I wanted to help your mother, but the bad woman wouldn't tell me where she was.'

Sienna looked at Feng in astonishment. She felt a thrill – like a bolt of electricity – pass through her. 'Bad woman? Do you mean Ling?'

Feng nodded. 'She was your mother's assistant.'

Sienna took a deep breath. 'Tell me what happened the day my mum disappeared.'

He took a sip of his tea. 'The last time I saw your mother, Gege and Ling were with her in Pingdingshan. Gege was your mother's driver. He often picked her up from her hotel and drove her to the temple.' Feng looked Sienna in the eye. 'One evening, four months ago, Gege didn't come back. I waited in front of the hotel for him, like I did every day. Then Ling came, in a taxi. I asked her about Gege. She said he was going to show your mother other temples and would be away for a while. I went to the hotel every evening, but he didn't come. Your mother didn't either. I came here, to Shanghai, to find this woman, to see if she could lead me to Gege. I've been watching her for weeks, but I still don't know what's going on. I thought you might be able to help.'

The room fell silent. Sienna was reeling at this information. Surely this must mean that Gege and her mother had been together when they disappeared. Somehow it was comforting to think her mum hadn't been alone.

Rufus was the first one to break the silence. 'Why don't you look in the box? There might be something you've missed, given this new information? Or the boy might spot something?'

Sienna looked down at her hands. She realized she hadn't let go of the tin box since she'd run out of the flat. Wordlessly she opened the box and laid the contents on the floor. The three of them looked at Sienna's treasures. She showed Feng the picture of the driver in the brown car. 'Is that your brother?'

He nodded, his eyes dampening. 'That's him, that's Gege.'

Rufus peered at the picture in Feng's hands. 'And that's Ling in the back! I should have known,' he growled crossly. 'First this woman is swanning around Henan with your mother, and now she's here, keeping an eye on you! That's no coincidence.'

Sienna's mum must have trusted Ling, told her about Sienna and her dad, about the flat in Shanghai. She felt a stab of anger at Ling's betrayal.

Taking a deep breath, she asked, 'Feng, do you think Gege is still alive?'

Feng glanced at the door, then turned to face Sienna. He looked defiant. 'I *know* he's alive. I'd feel it if he wasn't, wouldn't I? He's my brother.'

Sienna's head was swimming. Feng was right. Deep down, in spite of her dad and the counsellor and everyone else telling her to accept her mother's death and move on, she'd never really *felt* that her mum was dead.

Busy with her own thoughts, she didn't notice someone climbing quietly through the open window into the house. The new visitor had already made herself comfortable on the windowsill and was observing proceedings. With an air of disdain she washed her face with her dainty paws.

It was only when she heard the tinkling of a bell that Sienna looked up. There sat a pretty white cat, a little bell hanging from her blue collar. Sienna knew immediately who she was: Minka, her mother's invisible friend.

怪物

6 Guaiwu - Monster

'**R**ufus Archibald Henry. I might have known you'd be causing trouble again.' The cat's voice was deeper than Sienna had expected.

Sienna looked at Rufus. She heard him growl softly. 'Minka Drusilba. It's been a long time since I chased a cat up a tree.'

Minka blinked once and the tip of her tail twitched, just a little.

'You two know each other?' asked Sienna.

'Yes, we do,' said Rufus. 'As a rule I have nothing to do with animals of her kind. In this case the contact couldn't be avoided, though; we lived in the same house, so to speak.'

'Oh, Rufus, I haven't got time for your nonsense,' Minka spat. She lowered herself gracefully from the windowsill and stalked across the room towards Sienna. She jumped on to the table. Rufus watched her suspiciously.

Feng was staring at Sienna. 'More invisible animals?' he asked.

The boy's tone reminded Sienna of how her dad spoke about Rufus. She hoped Feng didn't think she was making it up, or being silly. 'Yes, just one more,' she said, defensively.

The boy stared hard at Sienna, blinked, and dropped his eyes. He probably felt left out, Sienna thought, feeling sorry. He continued to search through the contents of Sienna's box.

'Who's the boy?' asked Minka, her ears pricking in Feng's direction.

'He's Feng. He can't see you or Rufus,' Sienna explained.

'Oh, I see.' Minka yawned and washed her whiskers. She scrutinized Sienna. 'Uncanny, the similarity – her eyes are the only thing you didn't inherit. Do you know who I am, or has she kept me a secret?'

Sienna looked at the cat's pale blue eyes. 'You're Minka. My mother told me about you. You were her cat when she was little. You're invisible, like Rufus.'

Minka's fur bristled slightly and her tail twitched. 'What do you mean, "were"? I *am* your mother's cat, even if your mother has decided to shut me out of her life. You humans are strange. As if friends could just dissolve into thin air!'

Sienna was about to respond, but Rufus was quicker. 'Minka,' he said. 'You can't blame Sienna for her mother's mistakes. And seeing as you place so much value on old friendships . . . I take it you know what's happened to Sienna's mother?'

Minka bowed her head a little. 'I'm sorry, I didn't mean to offend anyone. It's just a little hurtful. Anyway, Kate and I haven't had any contact in such a long time – not my fault, naturally – and then suddenly about a week ago—' The cat paused and began to lick her paws.

'WHAT?' cried Sienna. 'What happened a

week ago?'

'Well,' continued Minka, 'I had the feeling that she was calling me, that she needed my help. And yet I can't seem to find her. Strange, isn't it?' She looked at Sienna questioningly.

'Well.' Rufus cleared his throat. 'I'm sorry to have to tell you this, but Sienna's mother has disappeared without a trace. She was last seen months ago here in China, in Henan Province. To be honest, we don't even know if she's still alive.'

Sienna expected a reaction from Minka to this news. But Minka just lay down, her tail flicking. 'Rufus, you nitwit, do you seriously think I wouldn't know if she was dead? We special animals have a sixth sense – especially when it comes to our friends.' She turned to Sienna. 'Your mother *is* alive. Nevertheless, I think she's in danger.'

A surge of hope and happiness rushed through Sienna, so strong she could barely breathe. 'We've got to help her!' she cried. 'Where is she?'

'What's happening?' Feng asked Sienna, pushing the photos and printouts aside. 'Is my brother all right?'

'I don't know about your friend's brother,' said Minka. 'Kate's too weak to call me, and I can't find her on my own. We have to work together. There's no time to lose.'

Sienna sat down on the floor and rested her head on her hands. Was there *really* a chance of finding Mum?

'What's happening?' Feng repeated quietly. 'Are you OK?'

Sienna tried to explain, in a mixture of English and Mandarin.

He still looked a bit confused, but the boy clearly trusted Sienna . . . *and* believed her about the invisible animals, despite his misgivings. Sienna felt a rush of gratitude.

'I'd love an invisible friend,' Feng sighed. 'I used to have dreams when I was much younger, that I had a little dragon. Xiaolong was his name . . .' His smile faded. 'He was my very best friend. But when my mother died and Gege and I lived on the streets, those dreams stopped.'

Sienna saw such sadness in Feng's face as he spoke, but Rufus seemed unmoved. 'We need a plan,' the little spaniel said. 'Sienna, perhaps we should try to contact your father and tell him about what Ling was up to with your mother's jewellery?'

Sienna didn't bother asking Rufus how he knew about the incident with the jewellery, when he hadn't even been there! Invisible friends could be very mysterious . . . Pulling her mobile phone from her pocket, she dialled the only number in her contact list – Dad's. Again, the same recorded message as she'd heard earlier in the flat. It was no good: she couldn't get through.

Feng picked up a photograph from the pile on the floor. It showed a Chinese pagoda, painted in red and gold. 'This is the Fragrant Mountain Temple. Our temple. This is where your mother worked, and where she met Gege.'

'Oh! That's where Kate called me from – I know it is.' Minka said.

'How do you know she called you from there?' asked Sienna. 'Could you be mistaken?'

'You know how I always manage to find you when you need me the most? I can feel where you are,' said Rufus.

'Then why doesn't Minka know exactly where my mother is *now*?' Sienna cried.

'Calm down, princess. Your mother and Minka hadn't had any contact in a long time,' Rufus explained. Then he smirked. 'Besides, cats naturally don't have such a distinct sense of place as dogs.'

Minka hissed. 'Nonsense. Anyway, enough talking. It's high time we were on our way.'

'This temple is in Henan, and that's hundreds of kilometres away. How will we get there?' asked Sienna, feeling dizzy at the speed at which things were happening.

Feng stood up. 'We can get the night train,' he exclaimed. 'But Ling will be looking for you. You'll have to be disguised.'

Sienna felt the crumpled money in her jeans pocket. A few notes – enough for cheap clothes from a street stall, perhaps, but not for two train tickets. Her face fell.

'Don't worry,' said Feng. 'I've saved my wages from the cookshop. Between us, we'll have enough.'

Rufus sighed. 'If I'm going to travel by train in this country, it'd better be first class,' he muttered darkly.

Sienna snorted. 'As if!' She turned to Feng,

deliberately ignoring Rufus's grumpy growl. 'OK, we'll do it.' Looking at him standing right next to Minka and Rufus, she sighed suddenly. 'Oh, I wish you could see Rufus and Minka. It would make things so much easier!'

Rufus looked thoughtful. 'Well, it's interesting this one *can't* see me. I'm not trying to conceal myself from him.'

Minka twitched her tail. 'I'm not hiding myself from him either. Perhaps this one is older than his years – so even though we show ourselves, he really doesn't seem to see us.'

Rufus and Minka exchanged knowing glances. Sienna didn't understand a word they were saying! 'What does that mean? You want him to see you, but he can't? *Should* he be able to?'

'Yes, if we let him – he's only a child, after all,' muttered Rufus. He looked thoughtful, studying Feng with his head tilted to one side. 'He's had a tough life, this one. Nevertheless, he *does* still have a special friend – I caught a glimpse of him when the boy was daydreaming outside of the restaurant. But his friend isn't with him all the time, and he isn't here right now.'

Sienna looked over at Feng. She wanted to tell him what Rufus had just said, that he did have an invisible friend, just like he'd dreamt. But as she struggled to find the right words, Feng pointed to the clock on the wall. 'We must go. The night train leaves soon!'

The sky above them had turned black, but it wasn't only the dusk that shrouded the little alley in darkness. A storm was brewing. Sienna had bought some cheap clothes from a stall near the house, and was wearing a long dark skirt, a floral blouse and a headscarf. The unfamiliar material felt strange on her body.

She and Feng each carried a small, battered holdall containing some water and spare clothes. Feng had packed an extra bag with food, which he had gone out to buy while Sienna had been changing. Rufus and Minka had made themselves comfortable on the bags, both of them grumbling quietly: 'Stop that jolting. Hey, careful on the bends!'

As they emerged from the narrow alleys and back on to one of the main streets, the first drops of rain started to fall.

Minka miaowed indignantly, as though someone had trodden on her tail. 'Rain! Put the
umbrella up now. NOW! My fur's getting wet!'

Sienna opened the umbrella that Minka had
insisted they bring. Feng watched her with a
puzzled smile on his face – the rain didn't seem
to bother him at all.

The pavement was crowded with people
trying impatiently to get to the other side of the
main road. Sienna took care to balance the
umbrella and the bags. The little group now
found themselves surrounded by people, all
hurrying at a fast pace towards the station. The
roads were jammed with cars, taxis pulled up at
the kerb and motorcycles squeezed their way
through the heavy traffic. Sienna felt overwhelmed by the noise and the heat.

A loud bang sounded overhead. Everybody
looked up, startled. Then there was a blinding
flash in the sky, and rain poured down on the
city as if someone had turned a shower on at full
strength. Umbrellas bowed under the weight of
the water.

'Quickly!' cried Feng, and they dashed the last
few metres towards the station.

'Made it!' gasped Sienna as they burst into the huge, brightly lit building.

Feng left Sienna and went to buy two train tickets. 'These were the cheapest ones,' he explained when he returned. 'Now I have no more money. But at least we will be on our way to find Gege and your mother.'

The friends forced their way slowly through the crowds. The air was warm and moist, and the scent of fried food hung in the air.

Suddenly all of the children and babies on the platform began to scream and cry. Sienna looked in amazement at the children, whose parents were trying desperately to calm them down.

As one, Rufus and Minka leapt from the holdalls, fur standing on end and staring wildly back towards the entrance to the station.

Feng was looking around uneasily at the crying children. 'What's going on?' he asked.

'I don't know,' Sienna replied. But then she saw it. At first she only glimpsed a head, which towered above the crowd, and her breath caught in her throat.

'What can you see?' said Feng, noticing the change in her expression.

It was a crocodile – or some sort of crocodile beast. Its eyes shone a poisonous yellow, and sharp white teeth flashed in its cavernous mouth. It was behind them, moving at a leisurely pace towards the train, and it was walking upright on two legs, like a person.

Sienna knew that this beast was invisible. Not to her – or to the babies and children, or the other invisible animals – but to the crowds that were now streaming through the train's open doors. Feng was staring at her face, eyes wide with confusion and fear.

The crocodile monster was getting closer and closer . . .

Sienna's legs felt weak, and she had to force herself to move. 'Feng, we have to run! We have to get on to the train!'

'Why, what is it?' he shouted, hurrying after her.

Sienna and Feng pushed through the crowd and eventually reached the train door. The monster had stopped some distance away and Sienna felt the tension in her chest relax a little as they climbed up into the carriage. She took a deep breath.

But where were Rufus and Minka? To Sienna's horror, she saw the invisible friends standing right in front of the monster, as if to protect her and Feng. The monster's mouth opened wide, its eyes glinting, a grating noise filling the air, and Sienna realized it was laughing. As if it had sensed her thought, the crocodile monster turned its head and fixed Sienna with narrowed, yellow eyes. She stumbled against Feng, who steadied her. And something else was suddenly clear to Sienna, though she didn't know *how* she knew: the creature had come for *her*.

'It's after *me*, Rufus!' Sienna screamed from the open train doorway, regaining her senses. 'Run away! Minka, Rufus, run!' But if they heard her, they ignored the command. Other passengers stared and muttered, but Sienna barely noticed.

The train's engine rumbled to life. Sienna clutched the bar beside the door and stared as the two brave creatures moved in for the attack: Minka's back was arched and she was hissing wildly. Rufus was snarling, his body tensed. Both animals looked so small in comparison to the crocodile monster.

Suddenly Rufus launched himself at the crocodile's leg, teeth bared. In one oddly elegant movement, the monster swept the little dog aside and knocked him across the ground, whimpering.

'Rufus!' Sienna cried.

Minka lashed out with her sharp claws, quick as lightning, but the crocodile was even quicker, a well-aimed punch sending the white cat tumbling in a ball of snarling fur. The crocodile fixed its eyes on Sienna again, as if in triumph, and her heart stopped.

At that moment, the train door closed. Sienna lost sight of Rufus and Minka for a moment. When she looked desperately back through the window as the train pulled away, the crocodile monster was still staring right at her.

And in its claws, held by the scruff of their necks, were Rufus and Minka.

大夫

7 Daifu - Doctor

Feng pulled her back into the train compartment. Although he hadn't been able to see the crocodile beast, or the fight with Minka and Rufus, he understood that something terrible had happened. He stuffed the two bags under the seat and pushed Sienna gently on to the bench beside him. Then he took her cold, trembling hand and whispered softly to her, 'It's OK, it's OK.'

The other people in the compartment openly

studied the strange pair, but Sienna couldn't care less! Could invisible creatures die? If so, she was sure Rufus's and Minka's lives were in danger. And if anything happened to them . . . she couldn't think straight.

Besides, if anyone could find her mother, Minka could.

Sienna felt Feng's warm hand on hers and finally met his questioning gaze. Using a mixture of English and Mandarin, she explained what had happened as best she could. Feng looked wordlessly at her, the colour draining from his face.

The rain pattered against the window. The train moved slowly and squeakily along the tracks. Sienna looked out of the window, the tears that were welling up in her eyes blurring her vision. She blinked and they started rolling down her cheeks.

'*Shoupa, yao bu yao* – would you like a hand-kerchief?' An old man sitting opposite them held a neatly folded white handkerchief out to her.

'*Bu yao* – no, thanks,' she mumbled quietly.

The man leant across to her. 'You know,

sometimes one thinks one has lost everything and cannot go on, but you must have faith. Perhaps this train is taking you to the right place.'

They travelled on through the night. Luggage was crammed into the racks above their heads, and the passengers sitting underneath were squashed together just as closely. Some were already asleep, others were absorbed in books or newspapers, and lots of them were eating. The smell of dried meat and fish reminded Sienna of breakfast with Ling that morning. It felt like years ago that she had been sitting with her in the kitchen.

The old man sitting opposite smiled as he glanced at Feng's T-shirt. '*Xiangshan Si?* Fragrant Mountain Temple?'

Feng looked up in surprise and nodded.

Sienna studied the man closely. His eyes seemed kindly, although his voice was low and serious. 'That's a very long journey you're making. I hope you're prepared for such a trip.'

Sienna was so tired it took her a moment to realize that she understood almost everything the man was saying. She squinted at him. There seemed to be a shining energy surrounding him, like tiny glittering dust particles, and she rubbed her eyes to try to clear her vision.

'Well, Feng knows the city we're going to well. And we have plenty of supplies with us,' said Sienna. She realized she was responding in sing-song, fluent Mandarin. *How did I do that?*

The man looked at her with a smile in his eyes and continued to speak in Mandarin, 'I don't know what you've got planned, but that was an ugly scene on the platform earlier. I hope you're not in danger.'

'What . . . what do you mean? Can you see . . . did you really see . . . ?' stammered Sienna.

The man smiled. 'Yes, I can see what you see. It gets harder every day, when one is getting older, but I'm still quite well practised. I can even see the little dragon that keeps flying around your friend's head.'

Sienna couldn't believe her ears. An adult who could see their invisible friends! And . . . a dragon? A little dragon . . . ?

She remembered Feng mentioning his childhood daydreams. Rufus said he'd caught sight of Feng's invisible friend, although he hadn't mentioned a dragon, and outside the restaurant, she had once spotted a flash of light over Feng's head – like a flicker of fire. Could it have been . . . ?

Concentrating as hard as she could, Sienna stared at the space above Feng. After a few moments, she saw him. As small and translucent as a bubble, a tiny dragon was trying desperately to attract Feng's attention. He was pulling Feng's hair with his tiny claws, and now and then he spat out small quantities of fire, flashing in the shadows of the carriage. That must be what she'd seen before! The little creature looked totally exhausted, and Sienna was afraid that he could come plummeting down at any moment.

Feng was looking at her quizzically.

'Above your head – a little dragon!' Sienna pointed. 'Just like you imagined when you were little!'

Feng whispered, 'Xiaolong,' then reached above his head, desperately trying to find the invisible creature. But his hands passed straight through the dragon, and eventually Feng dropped his hands to his lap, looking sadder than ever.

'We sometimes wish for the most wonderful friends when we're children,' the man said quietly to Sienna. 'It's a pity most people forget their special friends sooner or later, when the mind turns outwards and imagination lessens. You must concentrate hard and have faith to keep cherished companions.'

'Do *you* have a special friend . . . ?' asked Sienna. She couldn't help but ask – she'd never met anyone who knew of invisible friends before.

'Oh yes,' replied the old man, smiling warmly. 'He's been with us this whole time, and you in particular have already started to benefit from his presence! I think it's time we all introduced ourselves.' He nodded slightly to the children and kept his head lowered for a while. Then he said with a beaming smile, 'My name is Zou. And this here' – he put his hand into his jacket pocket – 'is Bai tuzi.'

'White hare,' whispered Sienna, frowning. She felt sure she'd never learnt the words in Chinese; they'd just popped into her head from nowhere. 'I'm Sienna, and this is Feng,' she added hurriedly, unable to take her eyes away from the creature sitting on Zou's hand.

Staring straight at Sienna was a small hare. He had sparkling red eyes and long, white fur. Most striking were his huge white ears, which seemed to glisten. A fine, sparkling dust hung in the air near the hare, giving him a magical, otherworldly appearance.

Zou stroked Bai's ears, his eyes twinkling. 'My friend is rather special,' he said. 'You may have noticed that you are finding it easier to master the complexities of Mandarin since you and I began to converse?'

Sienna nodded, her eyes wide.

'Well, that is one of his unique talents,' Zou smiled, continuing to stroke the hare's ears. 'It has to be said that Bai is rather a wonderful creature.'

Sienna turned to Feng to explain what was happening, but he didn't seem to be listening; he was staring forlornly out of the window at the passing countryside. Above his head the tiny dragon flapped around, looking very tired and miserable, his little coughs of smoke reminding Sienna of sobs.

Zou stood up and bent over Feng's head, and

in a lightning-fast movement he took hold of the dragon gingerly between his wings and held him in his hands. The frightened animal fluttered like a trapped butterfly. Carefully Zou sat back down in his seat. Now he raised his hands gently in front of his face. The dragon looked into the man's eyes and seemed to slowly calm down. Zou placed the dragon on his lap, where he fell instantly asleep.

The little hare made himself comfortable next to the dragon and studied Sienna and Feng with interest.

Feng looked with wide eyes at Zou and Sienna, who did her best to explain about the invisible friends.

'Your little dragon is already fast asleep,' she said.

Feng peered closely at Zou's lap, but he still couldn't see them. Frustrated, he closed his eyes and rested his head against the window.

'Let us try to find out more about this dragon, and why your friend cannot yet see him,' Zou whispered. 'Would you like to . . . ?' He gently scooped up the dragon and held his hands out towards her.

Sienna nodded, and he placed the tiny animal into her hands. The dragon was even lighter than she had expected. She laid him on her lap and covered him up with part of her skirt. Suddenly feeling utterly exhausted by the events of recent hours, she closed her eyes and fell into a deep sleep.

The first thing Sienna saw when she opened her eyes was a huge red sun coming up over the fields. Even the dirty train window couldn't spoil the view.

Glancing down, she saw that the tiny translucent dragon was still slumbering peacefully on her lap. Next to her, Feng stretched and, seeing she was now awake, asked impatiently, 'Where is my dragon? What's he doing? Why can't I see him? How can this man see him when I can't?'

'Ssh!' whispered Sienna, aware of the curious glances from the other passengers on the train. Zou himself was sleeping. 'The little dragon is asleep. And this man – Zou – can see all invisible friends, it seems. I don't know how. But I think we can trust him. Besides, he might be able to help us.'

Feng frowned and then peered out of the window again. 'We're nearly there,' he announced. 'This is Pingdingshan!' His voice woke Zou, who gazed bleary-eyed at the view.

The train was moving even more slowly now and Sienna could see that they had reached some sprawling suburbs. The passengers were stirring; people were hunting for their luggage, tugging it down from the racks on to the floor, and the great jostling match to be first off the carriage had already begun.

At the other end of the carriage she spotted a guard in a dark green uniform. He was leaning over one of the passengers, an elderly Chinese woman, who was speaking to him animatedly. She was looking in Sienna's direction, and now she pointed to her too.

The man looked at Sienna and Feng sternly. He came towards them, and suddenly Sienna realized that he wasn't a guard – he was a police-man! She felt her face grow hot and flushed. She stared down at the little dragon on her lap. She mustn't be discovered and returned to Shanghai: she had to find her mum!

Zou stood up and blocked the policeman's

path to Sienna. He told the policeman that Sienna was his goddaughter, who was now living in Shanghai. But then the policeman began to address his questions directly to her. The other passengers had stopped fiddling with their luggage and Sienna felt as though the whole of the train was staring at her.

Suddenly Sienna felt Bai sitting on her shoulder. The air seemed to be full of the glitter that covered his fur. She suddenly felt full of confidence. Turning to the policeman she bowed her head politely and said, 'Wo shi Pingdingshanren, zhu zai Shanghai – "I come from Pingdingshan, and I live in Shanghai."' She didn't recognize her voice any more. She sounded like a real Chinese girl!

After asking her how her journey had been and receiving a polite response, the policeman appeared satisfied. He wished Sienna a pleasant stay in the city with her godfather and disappeared, not forgetting to give the woman at the other end of the compartment a dirty look as he went.

Zou burst out laughing and Feng looked at her open-mouthed. The white hare nodded briefly to Sienna.

'*Xiexie* – thank you,' she whispered.

'*Buxie* – you're welcome,' Zou replied. 'As I said, Bai tuzi is a rather special hare and he loves his little performances! Now, time to get off the train. I suggest you two follow me; Bai tuzi believes we have our destination in common.'

Sienna and Feng looked at each other. Sienna meant what she had said to Feng: she felt they could trust Zou. Anyway, what were their options? Sienna was only twelve years old and she thought Feng was a bit younger. They had no money and nowhere to stay. They needed help to find her mother and Gege.

She also had to find out what had happened to Rufus and Minka. She hoped fiercely that they were all right – she didn't know what she would do without Rufus – and Zou seemed to know all about invisible friends.

Nodding at Feng, the two friends followed Zou off the train. Feng pulled both the bags behind him, while Sienna carried the small dragon – still fast asleep – carefully in her hands.

8 Long – Dragon

Sienna and Feng walked behind Zou through the dense crowd on the platform. Outside the station, Zou flagged down a rickety old green-and-white bus.

The new friends squeezed themselves inside. It was so overcrowded that they could hardly find room to stand. Sienna was afraid the little dragon might get crushed in her hand, but he seemed to be deeply asleep.

The bus jolted through the dusty city. Sienna

saw rows of small shops above which one-storey houses were stacked like tin boxes. In every garage it seemed someone was selling something, and all the streets looked the same. After a while the bus started to empty out and she gratefully slid on to one of the slashed plastic seats.

'We're here!' Zou finally announced. They got off the bus and Zou rummaged in his pockets for his key. He went to one of the small shops, which had a garage-style door, opened the lock and pushed the door up with a squeaking noise. 'Come in. I'll make some tea.' He smiled at Sienna and Feng, before switching the light on.

They looked around in amazement. Behind a wooden counter stood countless glass jars filled with leaves, roots and flowers. The shelves reached right up to the ceiling.

'These herbs are not used to make ordinary tea, but to prepare medicine. Ancient Chinese medicine,' replied Zou. 'So, now you can call me Doctor Zou too,' he said, giving them one of his radiant smiles. 'For you, young lady, I would recommend something to cool your blood! And for you, young man, something to clear the vision, perhaps?'

Feng frowned.

Sienna looked around the room for a safe place to put the small dragon down. She headed towards an armchair which stood alone in a corner next to the many shelves. As she opened her hand carefully, she felt a burning pain. 'Ouch!' she cried. The dragon was awake, and had apparently regained his strength: he spat out much more fire now than he had done on the train. 'What was that for?' cried Sienna.

The tiny animal flapped furiously up and down in front of Sienna, still breathing fire. Zou quickly picked him up and held him in front of Feng's face. Feng looked intently at Zou's hand, but he still couldn't see the dragon. Frustrated, he threw his bag on to the floor.

Zou turned to the invisible animal. 'Calm down, little one. We're all friends here. This young lady' – he turned the dragon to face Sienna – 'has taken very good care of you.' Then Zou pointed to Feng. 'Your special friend can't see you, for some reason. But I'm sure he will in due course. Now, I think we must all be hungry. I will prepare us some tea and food.'

Sienna rubbed her hand and Zou showed her

upstairs to a small bathroom where she ran cold water over the blistered skin to soothe the pain. She then whipped the headscarf from her hair. It was such a relief to take it off! Over the basin hung a small mirror. She had to stand on tiptoe to look into it. She looked at her reflection in shock – she hardly recognized herself: her uncombed fair hair hung in her face and her eyes seemed to shine more brightly.

Sienna shook her head. Everything had changed, and she felt that she had changed too! She knew now that the world was *full* of extra-ordinary people and invisible animals. And inside she felt alive with the hope that she was on the right track to finding her mum. Taking a deep breath, she washed her face and scraped her blonde hair back into a ponytail.

Turning into a room right next to the bath-room door, she saw that Zou was now frying some tofu and eggs in a pan, with a rice cooker bubbling on the floor. Sienna's tummy rumbled as she realized she hadn't eaten for almost a day! Feng was sitting at a table. He looked exhausted.

Sienna looked around the room. It was small

and sparsely decorated. Zou saw her curious glance.

'You must excuse my humble home,' he said. 'I'm not here very often. I go wherever I'm needed, so I'm usually away.' He grinned broadly.

Sienna smiled back at him. She felt as if she had known him for a very long time. Remembering that they had some food in the bags that they could contribute to the meal, she began to unpack.

'What have we here?' exclaimed Zou happily as he saw what Sienna was doing. He headed over to the table with plates for each of them piled with food. 'Mmm . . . moon cakes! My favourite! A sure sign that the Moon Festival is nearly upon us.'

'What are moon cakes?' asked Sienna, studying the small, round cakes Feng had bought, as she gratefully ate a mouthful of the tofu Zou had just cooked. 'And what is the Moon Festival?'

'You have been in this country for weeks and *nobody* has explained about the Moon Festival?' He shook his head despairingly at Feng – who shrugged – and sat down next to Sienna. 'The Moon Festival is one of the most important events in Chinese culture, also known as the mid-Autumn festival. It marks the time of the year when the moon shines the brightest, a time of great celebration when friends and family gather together to pray, feast and give thanks to the gods. The festival takes place in three days' time, when the moon is full.'

Feng sat up straighter in his chair, seemingly cheered by the mention of the Moon Festival. 'Moon cakes are always eaten around the time of the Moon Festival,' he explained. 'This is why I bought some. You must try one.'

The small round cakes were decorated with Chinese characters. Sienna bit into one. The sweet pastry tasted wonderful, but she was shocked to discover a salty egg yolk in the middle of the cake. Yuck!

'Ah yes, a hard-boiled duck-egg yolk,' said Zou, beaming. 'It symbolizes the full moon.'

Feng passed her another cake. 'Take this one instead,' he said. 'It's got lotus paste in it.' Sure enough, it was much sweeter. Feng smiled sadly as he saw Sienna enjoying the cake. 'Gege and I were planning on making moon cakes to sell at the temple,' he said softly. 'Many people will flock to the temple for the Moon Festival, to burn incense and light lanterns and celebrate the full moon.'

Sienna nodded, studying the picture of the pagoda on his T-shirt as Feng had just taken off his jumper. She could imagine how lovely it would be all lit up.

Suddenly Xiaolong, who had been sitting quietly on a shelf, shot at Feng like a rocket and started to spit fire at him, making him drop his moon cake. The dragon then looked intently at the cake and let out a strange cry.

'He's trying to tell us something,' Zou cried. 'What is it, Xiaolong?' The dragon, seeming much stronger than he had been on the train, lifted a trembling wing and pointed to the boy's T-shirt.

'What is it? What's happening?' cried Feng. He was rubbing his arms where the sparks had landed. Even though he still didn't seem able to see the dragon, he *could* feel the flames, Sienna realized.

'Is it the T-shirt?' asked Zou. 'It shows the temple, doesn't it?'

The little dragon nodded, but then fluttered

to stand on top of one of the moon cakes and uttered another strange cry.

Zou frowned. 'We already know we need to go to the temple, little one. But why are you so interested in the moon cakes?'

Something suddenly occurred to Sienna. 'The Moon Festival,' she cried. 'I think the little dragon is trying to make a connection between the festival and the temple!'

Xiaolong immediately fluttered up to Sienna and nestled close to her, as if to confirm she was right. She felt pleased but also confused. What did the Moon Festival have to do with the temple, and how was this connected to the disappearance of her mum . . . ?

寺庙

9 Simiao – Temple

The next morning, after a restless night's sleep, Sienna woke up determined to go to the temple right away. After Xiaolong's strange actions yesterday, and now knowing that the Moon Festival was only two days away, she was burning to find out if there really was a connection between the festival, the temple and the disappearance of her mum.

Zou had headed out at first light, saying he had urgent business to attend to. But, annoyingly, Feng had woken in a strange mood and seemed reluctant to help Sienna get ready for their journey. The little dragon had disappeared.

'Feng, we *need* to go to the temple,' Sienna insisted, for the third time. 'We've come all this way!'

'I'm *NOT* going,' he snapped, sitting on the floor with his head in his hands.

'What do you mean "not going"?' asked Sienna. 'That's why we're here! We need to find my mother and your brother. It's simple!' She missed Rufus hugely. With Feng in this mood, she felt very alone. 'Or don't you care about your brother?' she threw at him in frustration.

But this time, Feng didn't argue. He breathed out heavily and fell silent.

'Feng, what is it?' said Sienna, softening her voice. 'I'm sorry. I shouldn't have said that.'

'The temple . . . it's the place where Gege disappeared,' he said. He spoke very quietly now, his eyes filling with tears as he glanced up at Sienna and back at floor, as if ashamed. 'I know we should go but . . . bad things must be happening there. I'm afraid.' Feng swallowed. 'I can't go. I'm too scared of what might happen. Please don't tell Zou.'

Suddenly Sienna understood and her anger evaporated. She sat down beside Feng on the floor and took his hand. At that moment, Zou came down the stairs.

'Why are you both looking so sad?' he said. 'Shouldn't you be on your way to the temple?'

Feng opened his mouth to reply, but Sienna spoke instead. 'I've decided to go on my own,' she said. 'Only . . . I don't know the way.' She blushed, feeling a little foolish, but Feng glanced across at her gratefully.

Zou's eyes passed from Sienna to Feng and back again. 'Very well,' he said slowly. Somehow, he appeared to understand. 'Why not take Bai tuzi? He knows how to get there. He knows a surprising amount of things! And he can help you if you need to ask questions.'

Zou took the white hare on to his arm and stroked him affectionately. Sienna saw sparkly dust rise from the hare's fur into the air, and she glanced at Feng's glum expression. He was probably feeling guilty. She would be sorry to go without him, but she *had* to go to the temple.

'Thank you,' she said to Zou, standing up. Bai

tuzi hopped towards her, and she reached a hand out to stroke the animal's soft ears. Then she quickly got changed into her travelling clothes, hiding her blonde hair carefully under the headscarf.

The white hare and Zou nodded to each other, then Bai tuzi jumped on to Sienna's shoulder.

'That tickles,' she laughed, as the hare gently rubbed his nose against her ear. She waved good-bye to Feng, who was slumped in his seat, and went downstairs with Zou.

Sienna was glad when they finally reached the temple. The man she'd sat next to on the rickety bus had stared at her for the entire journey. Finally he started to bombard her with all sorts of questions, but luckily, with Bai tuzi by her side, she was able to answer. Eventually the bus driver called out the name of her stop and she jumped off, relieved.

The air was hot and dry, yet when she spotted the temple on a hill in the distance, a shiver ran down Sienna's spine. So this was where Mum had spent so much time. And this was where she might find out what happened to her. With a determined sigh, she began to climb the rocky hill.

She first spotted the pagoda of the temple. Several groups of people were gathered around with their tour guides, who held umbrellas up in the air. Making her way past the pagoda and the tourists, Sienna came to an inner courtyard. At its centre, an old well was sunk into the ground, surrounded by a crooked stone wall. A miniature pagoda protected it from the elements. Behind her was a hall with steps leading up to its entrance. The hall doors and windows were latticed with wooden carvings, and up on the roof Sienna could make out two red dragon statues. She stood still, studying the statues.

'Can I help you?' a voice behind her suddenly asked. Startled, Sienna whipped round. In front of her stood a young man wearing a yellow-brown robe. He was Chinese, but he had addressed Sienna in English. He eyed Sienna searchingly through his silver-coloured glasses.

'No . . . um . . .' she stammered. 'I'm just looking around.'

The monk smiled at her. 'Well, I have a little

time, so I can show you the temple if you like? My name is Hong Yi.'

Sienna nodded her agreement and they walked on through the crowds together. 'Why are there so many people here?' she asked Hong Yi.

'It's the holidays,' replied Hong Yi. 'But this is not "many". Especially when one considers the significance of this temple. Many more will flock here for the Moon Festival, in two days' time.'

They were now standing at the entrance to the main hall and Sienna, like the monk, took her shoes off before going in. Several golden Buddha statues stood before them.

'The temple is almost two thousand years old,' Hong Yi began. 'Although it has been destroyed and rebuilt several times over, the ground on which it stands is of great historical significance. Especially the well at the centre of the courtyard where I met you; that well has remained untouched for centuries.'

Hong Yi turned to a statue of a woman standing on the back of a dragon. Sienna looked thoughtfully at the golden figure. The statue seemed familiar to her.

'Do you know who that is?' asked Hong Yi. Sienna couldn't make out his features in the dim light of the hall. Only his glasses glinted on his face.

'I'm not sure, she looks like a princess,' replied Sienna.

'This is Guanyin,' explained Hong Yi. 'All Buddhists in China worship her, for she is the goddess of mercy. She helps people in need. Here, in this sacred place, Guanyin first revealed herself as a goddess in human form. But you are right. She was born as a princess and sacrificed everything for her faith.'

All at once Sienna saw the resemblance. The picture that Feng had given to her in the restaurant, back in Shanghai, was a picture of a statue of Guanyin!

Hong Yi gave her a thoughtful look. 'I assumed you would know more about the temple. Didn't your mother ever tell you anything about it?'

Sienna was taken aback. 'You know my mother? And how did you know I was her daughter?'

Hong Yi gave a sad smile. 'You look just like

her. And I knew your mother well. Her work was very important for the temple. It is a tragedy for us all that she is no longer here. I'm very sorry.'

Sienna swallowed.

Just then, she felt a tickling feeling in her ear. The white hare wanted to tell her something – she glanced at him, perching on her shoulder, and saw his pink nose twitching towards the left. Sienna turned and saw a very old man in a monk's habit shuffling across the inner courtyard.

'Come. I'll show you the rest of the temple,' the monk said softly.

Sienna followed Hong Yi back out into the courtyard, skirting round the well, her eyes meeting the old man's as he passed. He hesitated for a moment and then slowly approached. Hong Yi stopped and bowed before the older monk.

The old monk was bald, but his eyebrows were snow-white and his smile was kind. Sienna could see great sorrow and compassion in his face. He reached out and clasped her hand between his, his skin dry and warm. Sienna noticed a sprinkling of pure white dust on his fingers, which felt oddly rough and calloused for the hands of a monk.

He began to speak in a deep and soulful voice. At first Sienna couldn't understand much, but gradually the tickling feeling in her ear grew stronger as Bai tuzi translated.

'My name is Sun. It is such a pleasure to see you here,' said the old monk. 'It fills me with joy, and great pain too. Your mother was a very special lady. I wish I could ease your anguish.'

'Thank you,' said Sienna quietly.

Sun glanced over his shoulder, as if wary of the time. 'I must leave – I have important work to do and I should not leave my duties. It was my pleasure to make your acquaintance. I haven't given up hope that we will see your mother again, and I beg you not to give up either.'

I haven't, thought Sienna, and smiled. The old man bowed slightly and continued his walk, his broad shoulders stooped. Sienna felt over-whelmed by the old monk's words. It was hard to hold back the tears.

Hong Yi patted her shoulder gently. 'Your mother left some papers with us, the day she disappeared. Perhaps you would like them. If you wait here, I'll bring them to you. Will you be all right?'

'Yes,' she said, sitting down on the shaded steps. 'I'm fine.'

He nodded, and hurried off across the courtyard.

But Sienna wasn't fine. She felt sad and excited all at once – it was so confusing. She hoped Mum was OK, wherever she was – but Minka had said she was in danger. How would Sienna find her before it was too late? Bai tuzi pressed his nose against her cheek comfortingly. What papers could her mother have left here, and could they hide an important clue?

A moment later a loud gong pulled her from her thoughts. The door of another hall opened on the opposite side of the courtyard. A group of about fifteen monks streamed out. Sienna looked at the faces of the young men in their ochre-coloured robes.

Then she saw him.

It was the piercing blue eyes that gave him away, though he was also much plumper than the other monks. Pearls of sweat glistened on his brow. In his hands he held a golden vessel, which flashed in the sunlight. Sienna realized that the last time she had seen this man, in the apartment in Shanghai, something else had been flashing in his hand: a knife.

This was Ling's accomplice!

Desperate to get away before the monk recognized her, Sienna raced across the inner courtyard.

She was approaching the exit when someone gripped her arm. She jumped violently.

'What's the matter? Here, I found them.' Hong Yi handed Sienna a folder full of papers and pushed his glasses up his nose. 'These belonged to your mother. You should have them. But also I wanted to invite you here for our Moon Festival celebrations. It will be a *very* special occasion this year. And we are planning to say a special prayer for your mother.'

Sienna's heart was pounding. 'Um, thank you. I'll think about the Moon Festival. Thank you for showing me around. I have to go now.'

Waving a hasty goodbye at Hong Yi – who seemed a little hurt – Sienna raced down the mountain. The white hare whispered directions in her ear: *next right, next left, cross this road, that's the bus stop over there.* Finally she was sitting on the bus, feeling relieved, sweat tricking down her neck.

By the time she made it back to Zou's place, it was dusk. As she pushed open the door, she heard a familiar voice, and her heart began to thump violently.

活着的

10 Huozhede – Alive!

'My delicate nose simply cannot bear this smell. Thanks for your trouble, Doc, but I'm afraid I must stop this treatment.' There, right in front of Sienna, lying on a white cloth, was Rufus! Zou was standing over him, pouring a steaming drink into the dog's mouth.

'Waah!' wailed Rufus. 'Help! He's trying to poison me!'

'It's all over now,' the doctor soothed him. 'That was just some medicine to help soothe your energy and repair your good temper.'

Zou's words made Sienna smile even more – she certainly wouldn't describe Rufus as *ever* having had a 'good temper'! But she had never been more pleased to see her friend. She lifted Rufus from the couch and hugged him tightly. 'Rufus, you're alive! You're *alive*!'

'Of course I'm alive, silly girl,' Rufus said crossly, but he looked pleased to see Sienna and he gave her a tender lick on her nose. 'That monster had no chance against me.'

Sienna carefully carried her friend up the stairs, kissing and hugging him tightly, while Zou watched them go with a small smile upon his face.

Upstairs, the kitchen was empty and neither Feng nor Xiaolong were anywhere to be seen. Sienna had no time to wonder about that – she just wanted to know what had happened to Rufus.

'Where have you been? And where's Minka? Is she all right?'

'One thing at a time,' grumbled Rufus. 'The cat is fine. I'm glad she's not here. She never stops talking about herself.'

Sienna sat Rufus on her lap and stroked his fur gently. 'But where is she now?'

'She suddenly said she could feel your mother more strongly. Then she went off to look for her. Don't worry. She's tough, that one.'

Sienna rested her head against the little spaniel's head and tried to stop tears of relief from falling on his soft fur. 'But where have you been, Rufus? I saw you . . . it looked like you were dead!'

'Dead? Dead?! Me? Don't make me laugh!' scoffed the little dog, giving Sienna a gentle nip as a rebuke. 'We invisible friends cannot be killed that easily! And certainly not by one of our own kind. It is true that we can be injured . . . but we will heal, given time and the continued belief of our human counterpart.' Rufus saw Sienna's confused look and sighed. 'You didn't really think I was gone for ever, did you?'

Sienna paused and then shook her head. She realized that he was right: even after witnessing the terrible scene at the station, a part of her had felt that Rufus would be with her again.

'Well then,' continued Rufus firmly, 'it was the strength of your belief and your love that kept me alive. It's the same for Minka. Even though your mum claimed to have stopped believing in her, she never truly did. As long as you're here for us, we will *always* be here for you.'

Sienna smiled. She didn't think she would ever understand the mysteries of the invisible friends! Then her smile faded. 'But the monster, Rufus. Will the monster be able to find us again?'

'That's quite possible, Sienna. I take it you know who it belongs to?'

Sienna gulped and nodded. 'I think it's Ling's. Can Ling see you, Rufus?'

'Yes. And now we've met her best friend. A charming fellow, that monster. Now, come to think of it . . . where's *your* new bestie? Did the two of you have a falling-out? I know you're not always easy to get along with . . .'

'Rufus, stop it. I don't know where Feng is right now either. He couldn't come with me to the temple today.' Then Sienna told Rufus Feng's story about his brother, the Moon Festival, and her visit to the temple.

Rufus rubbed his nose thoughtfully. 'I am sure you are right. Something *must* have happened at the temple. Perhaps your mother discovered something that Ling wasn't happy about. But I don't know what part your new friend and Gege play in all this. Perhaps Feng knows more than he has told you? But I don't want you to get your hopes up too high; I've experienced first-hand what Ling and her crocodile companion are capable of.'

'Was it that bad?' asked Sienna.

'Pretty much. They asked constant questions about you and your family and whether Kate had been in touch and what she had told you. It was most dull. And that crocodile monster has the most evil bad breath. Not to mention the constant caterwauling from Minka . . .' Rufus shook himself. 'It's a wonder I survived, frankly!'

'Ah, I see you are feeling better.' Zou had come upstairs. 'Thanks, in no small part, to my potion, I expect!'

'You must be a very good doctor,' said Sienna, frowning at Rufus as he stuck his tongue out at Zou.

Zou put his head on one side and smiled. 'I don't know if I'm a good doctor, but I see things that other people don't. That helps a lot. Now, tell us what happened at the temple today.'

Sienna described everything that had happened, including the invitation from the monk to join them for the Moon Festival celebrations. Zou's eyes shone with pride when Sienna told him how the hare had helped her to find her way to and from the temple.

'A childish dragon and now a sparkling hare, this just keeps on getting better,' grumbled Rufus.

'Let's get some sleep,' said Zou, ruffling Rufus's fur. 'Tomorrow is another day.' He glanced at the sky through the tiny kitchen window. 'It's almost a full moon. And the day after tomorrow is the Moon Festival.'

As Zou laid mattresses out on the floor, Sienna thought again about where Feng and Xiaolong might be.

'Do you think he's all right?' asked Sienna.

'Don't worry,' Zou replied. 'This is his home city, so he won't get lost.'

Sienna snuggled up to Rufus and felt herself drifting quickly into sleep. With the familiar warmth of her spaniel friend back by her side, she knew she could now find Mum – she was sure of it.

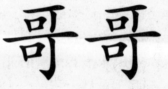

11 Gege – Big Brother

ienna was back in England. She was in her classroom at school, with Rufus. Everyone was staring at her. Mrs Kay, her maths teacher, seemed to be waiting for her to answer a question.

Rufus whispered the solution to her.

'Sorry, Mrs Kay. I think x equals five,' Sienna answered.

Mrs Kay frowned. 'Correct. But please stop talking to yourself now.'

Sienna realized she had been whispering with Rufus. The girls behind her giggled. She felt furious with them!

Suddenly Mum came through the door. Her face was dirty and her clothes were ragged. Her arms and legs were covered with scratches and mosquito bites. She reached out to Sienna. 'I miss you so much, my little one, please forgive me . . .'

Sienna wanted to jump up and to run to her mother, but a wall appeared out of the ground.

'Mum!' she cried. 'I can't reach you!'

Before the wall blocked her view, Sienna saw something white had appeared on her mother's shoulder.

It was Minka.

A delicious smell awoke her. On the kitchen table steamed a pot of hot tea, with *mantou* bread lying beside it. Rufus was snoring in her arms. Sienna placed the dog carefully on to the pillow and got up.

Zou greeted her cheerfully. 'Delicious dragon's head tea and warm *mantou*. Unless you'd prefer rice soup with dried meat.'

Sienna looked at Zou doubtfully. *Dragon's*

head tea?

'That's just what they call it,' explained Zou, seeming to read her thoughts. The doctor sat down beside Sienna at the table and bit into his bread. 'Now, whilst we were sleeping, Bai has been busy. There's still no sign of Feng, but Bai tuzi tells me he knows where he is. I think it's time we paid Feng a visit.'

Sienna hurriedly ate some bread and drank a slurp of tea. Then, after a quick visit to the bathroom, she tied the headscarf around her hair again. She was worried about Feng. He had seemed so sad yesterday when he'd told her about his fear of going to the temple. Plus she knew it was getting him down that he couldn't see his little dragon friend, or the other invisible creatures. Getting her things together, Sienna woke up Rufus. 'Time to get up, sleepyhead!' she whispered.

The dog got to his feet, grumbling. 'I'd rather stay here and sleep but I suppose I had better come with you – you'll only get yourself into difficulties without me. And they say humans are the most intelligent species. What a joke.'

They were about to go downstairs when

Sienna suddenly remembered the folder the monk had given her, containing her mother's papers. She dashed back to her room to fetch it. She had been so pleased to see Rufus yesterday that she'd forgotten all about it! She stuffed the papers in her bag, not wanting to be separated from them.

Outside the sun was up, but the almost-full moon could still be seen in the sky. Heat already blanketed the city Despite the beauty of the day, Sienna had an uneasy feeling, but she was tempted to take off the headscarf. Let people stare at her hair if they wanted to!

'It'd be better if you kept your disguise on. Where we're going, they've probably never seen a foreigner before,' said Zou, once again seeming to read her mind.

At the next crossing he ushered them off the bus. They were surrounded by modern blocks of flats.

'All newly built,' explained Zou. 'And still no one is living there.' He shook his head sadly.

Sienna followed him along the dirt road that wound between the apartment blocks. 'Where are we going?' she asked impatiently. Yellow dust coated her shoes and bag and she was hot and thirsty.

'It's not much further,' replied Zou. 'You see the stream back there?' He pointed to a muddy trickle of water.

On the opposite bank were some shacks built of wood and plastic. As they got closer to the water, an unpleasant smell filled the air. They crossed over the stream, using a few rickety wooden planks as a bridge. The stream was full of rubbish and waste.

'If I fall in, I'll never forgive you,' Rufus grumbled.

Zou stopped at one of the huts. 'This is it.' The hut didn't even have a proper door, just some plastic across the entrance. Sienna and Zou looked expectantly at Rufus.

'Hey, don't think I'm going to go first just because I'm invisible to most people. Out of the question!'

'Please, Rufus,' said Sienna. 'Can't you just have a quick look to see if Feng's in there?'

The dog disappeared behind the plastic curtain, muttering to himself. It wasn't long before he was standing in front of Zou and

Sienna again.

'Well, if anyone's interested, no dog would accept that kind of accommodation. The size of a shoebox, full of rubbish, and as for the smell . . .' Rufus shook himself.

'Just tell us, Rufus. Is he in there?' Sienna snapped.

'Oh, yes. He's fast asleep.'

Zou and Sienna went into the shack. The sun shone through the holes in the roof, and the only furniture was a plastic table, two chairs and a small wooden shelf with a hotplate on it. Clothes, cutlery and a few CDs were piled up on the floor. On a mattress in the middle of the room lay Feng. He was wearing a grey sweatshirt which was much too big for him.

Snuggled close by him, and also deeply asleep, lay Xiaolong. Sienna sighed with relief that they both seemed to be fine.

Zou shook Feng's shoulder. 'Time to get up, my young friend.'

Feng sat up with a start. He looked at his visitors, startled. Then he buried his face in his hands like a child hiding from strangers.

Zou clasped his wrists gently. 'I sense you are

carrying a heavy burden, young friend. I think it is time you told us everything,' he said softly.

Feng looked up at last. Tears welled up in his eyes and he took a deep breath. 'When my parents died,' he said quietly, 'Gege was my only family. I was just seven years old – Gege was fifteen – and we didn't want to go into a children's home.'

Sienna sat down next to Feng on the rotten mattress. Rufus remained standing at the door, scowling.

'We lived on the street for a long time. Gege did everything he could to take care of us, to find us a better life. Eventually, he found work in the mine nearby, but they closed down the pit. So we tried selling drinks and making ourselves useful at the temple, but it was difficult to earn enough to get by. The money Gege had saved ran out. Then we met a fat monk . . .' Feng paused and drew in a shaky breath. 'He saw us at the temple. He said he had some work for Gege. It involved a foreign expert who wanted to write a book about the temple. That was your mother, Sienna.'

Sienna swallowed hard at the mention of her

mum, then nodded at Feng to continue.

'The monk said Gege was to gain her trust. He had to help her with her work. He showed Gege a secret chamber behind the statue of Guanyin. All Gege had to do was make sure that your mother discovered it.'

'Why? Why didn't the monk just show my mother the chamber?' asked Sienna.

'The monk said your mother *had* to discover the chamber herself.' Feng rubbed his eyes. 'Gege liked your mother a lot, and he didn't want to lie to her, but the monk gave him a lot of money to do as he said. When your mother came across the chamber she was very excited. She said that what she had found there would be a sensation. It would make the temple famous.'

Sienna sat up straighter. 'So what did she find?'

Feng swallowed and paled. 'Something . . . something amazing. But Gege stole it from her. He said we would get a lot of money for it. That we'd be able to buy ourselves a proper flat, perhaps even a little shop. That was the day before he and your mother disappeared.'

'But what was it?' Sienna insisted, already half

guessing the answer.

Feng now stood up and walked outside to the bank by the stream. He pushed his hands into the soft brown clay and began to dig. When he had found what he was looking for he pulled out a mud-stained package and returned to the shack, panting. 'Here,' he said, and held out the package to Zou and Sienna.

Sienna carefully unwrapped it, and stared open-mouthed at the object. It was the brilliant-white statue from the photo that Feng had passed to her in the restaurant. Although not much bigger than Sienna's hand, it was much more impressive in real life. The stone was so white it appeared to sparkle in the sunlight filtering into the little shack.

'The moon princess,' Sienna cried.

Zou had sunk down to sit on the mattress. 'You're thinking of a different story, Sienna. This is the goddess Guanyin. So beautiful,' he breathed, and Sienna saw astonishment and adulation on his face. His eyes shone. 'But you're not *completely* wrong. Do you know the story of when she was a princess?' he asked, turning to Sienna.

Sienna remembered what the monk had told her yesterday. 'Only a little bit,' she said. 'Could you tell me the whole story please?'

'Guanyin was a princess indeed. She left her family to become a hermit. When her cruel father, the King, fell ill, she wept tears of mercy for him on the Fragrant Mountain on the night of the full moon. Despite his cruelty, she vowed to sacrifice her life for his. Guanyin's tears trickled into the earth at her feet and sank deep into the ground, a well of purest water springing from the spot. She died, but in sacrificing herself, saved her father. People realized she was actually a goddess – the goddess of mercy. The remorseful king buried his daughter at the summit of the Fragrant Mountain and built a pagoda on her grave, protecting the sacred well which had sprung from her tears. He had many more monasteries built and became a devout Buddhist.'

Rufus yawned and scratched himself behind one ear in boredom. 'Who cares?' he growled to himself.

'She was buried at *our* temple?' Sienna cried, suddenly feeling the pieces of the puzzle slot into place.

'Yes,' answered Zou. 'Although the temple has been destroyed and rebuilt many times, the well remains. It *is* the place where, according to legend, the goddess manifested herself.'

'What is all this rubbish?' Rufus shook himself vigorously, his long black ears flapping around. 'Guanyin . . . manifestations . . . temples. What this is really all about is that our friend here' – he threw Feng a hostile look – 'is telling us nothing but a pack of lies. Yesterday his big brother was a simple driver, today he's a cheat and a thief who deliberately deceived Sienna's mother. I vote the boy stays here and we go and look for Kate on our own.'

Sienna was glad Feng could neither see nor hear Rufus. She looked at her new friend's tear-stained face, his hair clinging to his cheeks. He looked so despondent, and she felt sure she could trust him, in spite of all the lies.

'Feng, have you told us everything now?' she asked him.

Feng nodded and sniffed noisily. 'Gege did help the fat monk, but he *didn't* know he'd put your mother in danger. Perhaps . . .' He hesitated. 'Perhaps they both disappeared because the statue is missing. Perhaps if we give the statue back then they'll be set free?'

'You may be right.' Zou nodded thoughtfully. 'Let's go home to my place, then we'll decide what to do. Feng, pack up the things you want to bring with you. This is no place for you.'

As Feng put a few things in a bag, Xiaolong woke up. He looked around the room and saw the statue in Zou's hands. He seemed happy, flipping around in the air and shooting sparks from his nostrils.

'Can you see him yet?' whispered Sienna to Feng, whose face was set in sudden concentration.

But he frowned and shook his head.

小猫

12 Xiao mao - Cat

It was late at night, and the floor of Zou's apartment was strewn with papers from the folder Hong Yi had given to Sienna. She was crouching amongst her mother's letters and research reports, searching for anything relating to the statue or Ling, while Feng had spread out the photos before him, and Rufus sat silently beside the boy, who had no idea he was there.

Xiaolong was sitting on Feng's shoulder. Sienna had noticed that he didn't seem to like being away from Feng nowadays, and was always on his shoulder or by his side. Sometimes Feng *almost* caught sight of the dragon, but the moments were almost as frustrating as they were fleeting. *Why can't I even see my own friend?* he would demand, his eyes swimming.

Sienna was trying to get her mother's notes into some kind of order to see if she could spot anything significant. She sorted all the documents by date, including all the letters and emails Mum had written. Her mother had arrived in China in March. The last anyone had heard from her had been a phone call in May. Now it was September. She sighed in frustration: she couldn't seem to find *anything*!

Suddenly there was a small sound from the ground floor, causing Rufus to sit up. Xiaolong flew up into the air and Sienna turned round just in time to see Minka come up the stairs with a series of elegant leaps. Her white fur was unkempt.

'Minka.' Rufus's voice betrayed no surprise. 'You're certainly not looking your best. I always thought you cats valued cleanliness, if nothing else. Clearly I was mistaken.'

Before Minka could reply, Zou came into the kitchen. He didn't seem at all surprised to see Minka. He greeted the cat with a friendly smile and a small bow. He warmed up some milk for her and placed a small bowl on the table.

Minka drank quickly, then jumped on to a chair and started to wash her paws. Sienna was bursting with curiosity. She knelt down by the chair.

'Minka, where have you been? Have you found my mother?' she asked.

'Of course,' the cat replied tartly. 'I told you back in Shanghai that she was alive, and now I've found her. You can always count on me.'

'She's alive!' Sienna repeated to Feng breathlessly. She sank down to the floor, feeling overwhelmed with happiness and relief. She wanted to laugh and scream and throw Rufus in the air!

Feng sat down beside her and stroked her arm gently. 'What about my brother?' he asked her. 'Can your . . . friend tell you about him too?'

Minka carried on cleaning her fur, as cool as a cucumber. The doctor and Bai tuzi watched her in fascination.

Rufus, though, had lost patience. 'Spit it out, will you? Where *are* they? What's happened to them?'

Minka sighed. 'Kate is being held prisoner, deep in a mine nearby. There is a man with her, though I didn't pay much attention to him, I'm afraid. I suppose he might be this one's brother.' She flicked her nose at Feng dismissively.

'Gege's all right too,' Sienna whispered to Feng. He smiled in relief.

Minka continued. 'She has other, very unpleasant company, though – that woman from the photos, whose fingernails are as sharp as the claws of her friend, the crocodile monster. Her voice could turn water to ice.'

'Ling!' cried Sienna.

'Yes,' said Minka. 'But the good news is, Kate is alive. She's writing a book, and she has until tomorrow to finish it. The witch has demanded it for the Moon Festival celebrations tomorrow night, apparently. After that, well, they won't need your mother any more.'

For a moment there was silence in the room. Sienna was trying hard not to think about what would happen when they no longer had any use for her mum. She wiped her eyes quickly with both hands and sniffed hard.

'I'll find my mum *and* Ling, and I'll make Ling wish she'd never messed with our family,' she said firmly. She sat down beside Minka and began to stroke the cat's fur carefully. 'Can you find your way back to where they're keeping Mum and Gege prisoner?'

Minka looked up contentedly to the ceiling as Sienna tickled her neck. 'But of course. There's only one problem – I can't get through to your mother. There were times when I thought she could hear me – she'd look in my direction, follow my movements with her eyes – but I also got the feeling she didn't want to speak to me.' Minka shook her head sadly.

'If you can find your way back to her, we should go right now,' Sienna said determinedly. 'We've got to get them out of there.'

'You're right,' said Zou, looking thoughtful. 'You should set out now. It'll be daybreak in a few hours.'

'Aren't you coming with us?' asked Sienna.

Zou shook his head. 'I'd only slow you down. I'll meet you at the temple for the Moon

Festival. Feng, take the statue with you, just in case. Rufus, I think you should stay with me. If anything happens, you'll be able to find your way back to Sienna and lead me to them.'

'I don't want to go without Rufus,' protested Sienna. She'd only just been reunited with him, after all!

'The doctor's right,' said Rufus, nuzzling her leg. 'Everything points to something big happening at the temple during the Moon Festival. You need to go with Minka and Feng to find your mother, and you've got to hurry. If you get into difficulties, I can come and find you.'

Sienna picked him up and hugged him tightly.

Zou led the small party downstairs. Opening a small iron door right next to the front door, he pulled out two rusty old bicycles. One of them was a delivery bike with a small basket between the front wheel and the handlebars.

'There you go,' said Zou with satisfaction. 'You should get there quickly on these.'

Sienna wheeled out the bike with the basket. Minka jumped inside with a huge leap, and the little dragon followed, keeping a safe distance from Minka, who hissed at him suspiciously.

Feng sat down on the saddle of the other bike. His feet barely touched the floor. Sienna hugged and kissed Rufus goodbye. She wanted to hug Zou, but instead held her hand out shyly.

The doctor gripped it firmly in his. 'Now it's up to you,' he said. 'You and Feng are strong, and you have two strong friends with you. Whatever happens, don't give up. And never stop having faith.'

Sienna swung herself on to her bike, and wobbled along behind Feng.

煤矿

13 Meikuang - The Mine

Despite the cool night air, riding the bike was hot work, and Sienna soon abandoned her disguise. She pushed the headscarf back from her face and hair, which clung to her skin in thick strands, and hitched up the long skirt, which kept getting caught in the pedals.

They'd been travelling for what felt like hours and were exhausted, the lights of their bikes throwing dizzy shapes across the road, but the prospect of finding their loved ones drove them on. Minka sat in the basket, showing them the way, while the little dragon slept.

They had left the city a long time ago, and the broad plains slowly gave way to a hilly landscape.

Suddenly Feng stopped. Sienna rode up to him.

'Have we gone the wrong way?' she asked Feng. Then she realized he was looking at a pale blue streak of sky on the horizon. Dawn. The day of the Moon Festival was breaking!

'To the left,' hissed Minka.

There was a small road among the trees, which the children followed as the sun rose steadily. Sienna was struck by how fresh the air felt. The city felt a million miles away – the roads no longer tarmac but packed dirt, the signs few and far between. She hadn't breathed woodland air since she had left England.

All of a sudden, the forest opened out. A collection of ramshackle buildings huddled in the clearing, a tall cylindrical tower at the centre. The windows of the buildings had been broken, and ivy was growing through the gaps. A dirty white van was parked outside.

'I remember this place,' Feng said, lingering in

the cover of the trees. 'Gege worked here a while ago. But it's been closed for years.'

Suddenly a tall man emerged from a door at the side of a small building.

'That's one of the guards,' hissed Minka. 'Take cover.' Feng and Sienna ducked behind a bush at the edge of the clearing, but the stranger was staring at the screen of his phone. After a few moments, he slipped the phone into his pocket and – muttering under his breath – climbed into the van. After a few moments, the engine sputtered to life and the guard drove away.

They waited until the noise of the engine had sunk into the distance. Sienna was glad the guard had left, but still worried about the task ahead. 'How are we going to find them?' she said, standing up. 'The mine is sure to have lots of tunnels and caves! They could be anywhere.'

'I can sense your mother,' said Minka. 'We'll find our way.' And the white cat padded to the low building the guard had left.

Sienna took a deep breath and glanced at Feng. He nodded grimly. 'Come on,' he said. The little dragon let out a miniature roar of determination.

Together the four friends crossed the sandy ground towards the entrance to the mine. The door was secured with a padlock. Sienna tugged as hard as she could but the lock held fast. 'There must be another way inside,' she said, frustrated.

'Wait here,' said Feng. He disappeared briefly and returned with a small piece of wire in his hand. He worked it inside the lock and had opened the door within a few seconds.

'Where did you learn to do that?' asked Sienna, wide-eyed. Feng just shrugged and pushed the heavy door open. They were in a dark, cramped hall.

Sienna and Feng spotted a tap and drank thirstily before walking across the hall. They found themselves standing in front of a latticed cage.

'That's the lift that runs down to the mine,' said Feng.

Minka nodded. 'They must have taken your mother and Gege down there in it.'

Sienna suddenly felt scared. She turned to Feng. 'If anything happens to one of us, the other one has to carry on the search for mum and Gege, right? Then we take them to the temple to meet Zou and find out what's going on. Agreed?'

He nodded and the two friends hugged. Then they turned to the lift.

Beside it stood a number of torches. 'Let's take a few of those with us,' said Feng. They took a torch each and got into the lift. Feng closed the door and pressed a button. The cage squeaked and creaked, and then, with a huge jolt, the lift was hurtling downwards.

It seemed to Sienna that the journey went on for ever. It was pitch black when they finally stopped and got out. She switched on her torch, illuminating a small room. There were two tunnels leading into darkness.

'Along here,' said Minka, and the little white cat led them into the tunnel to the right. There was no discernible end, and the further they travelled, the narrower it got. Sienna could only just walk upright, and she had the feeling that the huge weight of stone and earth above could collapse on her head at any time.

Suddenly a mountain of black rubble loomed in front of them, reaching up to the ceiling.

'They're nearby, beyond this rockfall,' said Minka, swishing her tail in frustration. 'We'll have to try a different route.'

But Sienna, desperate to reach her mother and knowing she was so close, fell to her knees and began to dig with her bare hands. 'We're nearly there,' she said. 'We can't stop now.'

Feng joined her, scraping away at the coarse, rocky earth.

The friends dug and dug, until their hands started to bleed. Meanwhile, Minka and Xiaolong tried to find another way through, Minka sniffing and pawing at the walls, the little dragon shooting sparks as he flew in circles overhead.

'Shine your light this way!' called Minka after some time. 'I've found something.'

Sienna straightened up and aimed her torch at the cat. The beam fell on a small opening in the tunnel wall. 'We might be able to crawl through there – perhaps it'd get us past the fallen stones,' Sienna said, and quickly disappeared on all fours into the opening.

Feng had no choice but to follow her.

But the tunnel grew narrower and narrower . . .

'We have to turn back, or we'll get stuck,' said Feng.

'Wait! I think it's opening up.' Sienna pushed

herself onwards as the tunnel widened. 'Come on,' she said to Feng.

'I'm not sure about this!' called Minka from behind. Her voice sounded very far away. The two invisible friends had lingered further down the tunnel. 'I have a bad feeling. Please come back, Sienna! We will find another way, I promise.'

Sienna knelt down on the floor to catch her breath. She couldn't give up, with Mum so near! As she rested, her mind swimming, she noticed something odd about the tunnel walls. Although dirty, glimpses of white shone here and there under the beam of her torch. She reached out and scratched away the earth nearby with her fingernail – a small moon-like crescent revealed the stone of the tunnel beneath, sparkling white and slightly damp to the touch.

Pure white: just like the statue. Just like the dust on Sun's hands. Just like moonlight.

But before Sienna could finish the thought, the tunnel began to shake and they heard a squeaking noise. 'What's that?' she asked.

'Sounds like the lift,' Feng replied. Small clumps of earth began to fall from the ceiling on to their heads. 'We have to go back!' he yelled.

But it was too late! Stone and gravel fell down from the ceiling and crumbled from the walls. Sienna and Feng huddled together and held their hands over their heads as more earth also hammered from the ceiling behind them.

The whole thing was over within seconds.

'Minka? Xiaolong?' cried Sienna.

Silence. A wall of rubble separated the children from the invisible friends.

Feng glanced at her anxiously. 'What is it? What's wrong now?'

'We're alone,' Sienna said simply, her voice hollow. She flicked the switch of her torch but it was dead, broken in the impact. They were alone in the dark and, worst of all, they were separated from Minka and Xiaolong. Now they had no way of knowing how to reach her mum and Gege *or* how to get out of the old mine.

Trying to swallow her feelings of panic, Sienna felt her way along the passage in the other direction, only to find it blocked in front of them too. 'We're trapped!' she said. She tried to think, her heart pounding in her ears. There was nobody to help them, and they were deep in a mine, a rockfall at either end of the tunnel. Although . . . what if . . . ?

A vague plan started to form in Sienna's mind. Would it work? *Could* it work . . . ? Turning to Feng, she started to speak. 'We are in real danger,' she said, trying to keep the tremble out of her voice. 'We only have one chance to get out of here. You have to call Xiaolong: make him use his flames to blast through the rockfall and get to us.'

'But he's so small!' Feng sounded doubtful.

'He's getting stronger each day. You have to believe in him. I know he has the power to do this. I can see him, but I can't summon him. Only *you* can do that.'

Feng hesitated. Then he gave a small nod and closed his eyes. After a few moments of silence, Feng opened his eyes. 'It's not working!' he cried in frustration.

'You can do it, Feng! Believe in him.' Sienna closed her eyes too and pictured the little dragon breathing a huge fireball, blasting through the rubble. She realized that it was getting harder to breathe: the air was running out!

Suddenly they heard a faint noise. It sounded

like roaring. 'I can hear that,' murmured Feng. 'But what is it?'

There was another roar and then a cloud of black dust fell over the children. 'Oh no, not another collapse,' whispered Sienna.

Then there was a flash of light and fresh air filled the small space where Feng and Sienna crouched. More soot fell. When it cleared, Sienna opened her eyes and saw that the rockfall had been destroyed, clearing space for them to make their way back down the tunnel. And there was Xiaolong, hovering in front of Feng. He seemed bigger, and *much* stronger.

To Sienna's amazement and delight, Feng reached out his hand and stroked the little dragon. 'I can see you!' whispered Feng, touching Xiaolong's snout tenderly. 'My friend, my little dragon.'

A noise from above caused Sienna to look up. As she did, she saw a large rock coming loose from the ceiling. 'Look out!' she shouted at Feng – but it was too late. She felt a sharp pain in her head and felt warmth spatter against her cheek.

Then there was nothing but darkness.

解救的

14 Jiejiude - Rescued

When Sienna opened her eyes she was lying on a bed. She turned her head to the side, aware that her head ached and was covered in a large bandage. There, sitting by her side, was a familiar figure. Dad!

Seeing that she was awake, her dad enveloped her in an enormous hug. She felt safe in his warm arms. 'Dad!' she croaked. 'You're really here. Am *I* really here? Where *is* here?!'

'You're in hospital,' Dad said softly. 'You're

fine, but you had a nasty knock on your head and you were very dehydrated.'

'But . . . but how did you find me?' asked Sienna. 'I was in the mine . . . the roof fell in . . . then I don't remember.'

'A huge part of the mine collapsed,' said Dad, speaking in a low, soothing voice.

Sienna's heart clenched. Mum and Gege were in the mine – what if they'd been trapped, or worse?

Dad continued. 'A security guard heard the explosion and found you unconscious outside. He called for an ambulance. I had reported you missing after a call from Ling, so the hospital contacted me right away. I was already on my way here as the last sighting of you was of you boarding a night train to Pingdingshan.' Dad stroked her face softly. 'What on earth have you been doing, my darling girl?'

'I had to come here, Dad. Because of Mum.' Sienna sat up in bed. Her head throbbed. 'Dad, Mum was in the mine! Did they find her? Was Feng there?'

Dad frowned. 'Who is Feng? You were all by yourself, my darling.' His frown deepened, his eyes sad. 'When are you going to accept that your mother is gone?'

Sienna shook her head. 'Dad, you have to listen to me. Ling's a crook – she pinched Mum's jewellery. And Mum, she's—'

Dad interrupted her, his shoulders stiffening. Sienna could tell he was angry, even though he didn't raise his voice. 'Sienna, you need to calm down.'

'Dad!' Sienna cried, 'Listen! Ling knew Mum. She's connected with her disappearance. But Mum isn't dead. She's *alive*—' Sienna broke off. 'At least, she was still alive this morning. It's all connected with the statue and the tem—'

Dad's voice was harsh as he cut her off. 'Listen to me, Sienna. Your overactive imagination is putting you in danger. What on earth were you doing in a derelict mine? You've injured yourself and ended up in hospital – and it could've been so much worse!'

Sienna's eyes filled with tears. She hated being told off by her dad – but it *wasn't* her imagination. 'I'm telling the truth!'

All of a sudden, his anger crumpled. He pulled her to him and hugged her tightly. 'For God's sake,' he said, his voice barely more than a whisper, 'please stop this nonsense. I can't lose you too.'

Sienna held her tongue. It was no use: he would never believe her. 'Sorry, Dad,' she said quietly.

'I'm sorry too,' he sighed. 'Get some rest, Sienna. I'll come back soon with some supper.'

Kissing Sienna on the forehead again, Dad left the room. As soon as he did, Sienna swung her legs out of the bed and then stood up shakily. What had happened to everyone? Feng must have carried her out of the mine, she supposed. She hoped he was all right. She longed to know if he had found her mum and Gege.

Looking out of her window she saw that it was late afternoon. From the hospital, she could just glimpse the curved pagoda roof of the temple on the hill. Suddenly she remembered: it was the Moon Festival tonight! Everything was coming together, and there was no time to lose – she had to go to the temple and find out what had happened. *Sorry, Dad*, she thought. *But I have to go. I have to find Mum.*

As she put her shoes on and grabbed her

clothes, still unsteady on her feet, a familiar voice exclaimed, 'Dearie me, don't you look a state! You could at least have brushed your hair.'

Rufus!

Gathering the little dog in her arms and inhaling his familiar scent, Sienna hugged him until he squeaked. 'Where have you been? Is everyone all right?' she demanded.

'Enough!' protested Rufus, struggling out of her grip. 'We'll meet Zou at the Moon Festival, as planned. I don't know about anyone else, but no doubt they'll meet us there too. Now hurry up. Hmm, I think I know the way . . .'

Feeling better already, despite the bandage round her head, Sienna followed Rufus out into the corridor and the lift. Now she had Rufus by her side, she knew she could make it through the town and back to the temple.

She just hoped she wouldn't be too late to save her mum.

艺术家

15 Yishujia – Artist

At dusk on the Moon Festival, the Fragrant Mountain Temple was busy with monks and visitors, preparing for the celebrations. Many of the monks were carrying fruit, flowers and other offerings in their arms. Their voices rose towards the moon, already a ghostly white disc against the deepening blue of the sky.

Sienna and Rufus blended with the gaggle of visitors at the temple gates, and hurried into the courtyard that had the well at its centre. A group of monks were finishing decorating the small pagoda over the well with flowers and strings of lanterns. Sienna turned away. She was terrified of spotting the fat, blue-eyed man a second time. The first time she had seen him, he had been wearing a suit. Then she had seen him in monk's robes. Was he really a monk? What would he do if he saw her? She couldn't forget that sight of the glinting knife clenched in his fist.

As Sienna passed the tree at the side of the courtyard, she heard a cry and glimpsed movement in the corner of her eye. She gasped and started backwards, heart in her mouth, her fists clenched, only to recognize Feng leaping out of the bushes. He almost knocked her over with the strength of his hug. 'Sienna! Are you OK?'

'Fine,' she said, laughing breathlessly, her pulse racing. 'Apart from the heart attack you just gave me.'

'Sorry.' He smiled sheepishly.

'Are *you* all right?' She remembered how he'd been too scared to visit the temple the previous day. 'It must've taken a lot of courage to come back here.'

'It's strange, but I feel braver now – I've been

trapped in a mine, so I think I can deal with a temple.' He grinned. 'And Rufus!' He caught sight of the little black spaniel and patted him on the head. 'I can finally see you!'

'We meet at last,' said Rufus, bored. 'Now if you'll excuse me, I'm exceedingly hot after that mad dash across town.' And with a yawn he settled himself in the shade of the tree and shut his eyes, his tongue lolling out of his mouth.

'Where's Xiaolong?' asked Sienna, searching the air above Feng's head.

'He and Minka stayed at the mine to search for Gege and your mother,' Feng explained, some of the light falling from his eyes. 'I haven't seen him since.'

Sienna bit her lip. 'What happened? Are Mum and Gege alive?'

'I think so. At least, Minka could still feel your mother after the rockfall. I managed to drag you out – I was so worried! But then the guard arrived and I hid in one of the outbuildings – I wanted to go with you in the ambulance, but I didn't want to leave Gege.' He looked ashamed.

'Never mind about that!' said Sienna, squeezing his shoulder. 'We promised each other to carry on searching, remember? What happened next?'

'I couldn't go back inside, after all,' said Feng. 'There were just too many guards around. But Minka and Xiaolong continued the search. So I came here to wait for Zou alone.' He shuffled on his feet. Sienna could tell he was worried about his little dragon. After all, he'd only just seen him for the first time in years, and now they were separated again.

'Don't be afraid for Xiaolong – invisible friends can look after themselves,' said Sienna, squeezing her friend's shoulder. *It's Mum and Gege I'm worried about*, she thought. 'Right now we need to find out more about that statue. I think I saw the stone it's made from in the mine – it was pure white, like marble, but almost glittery. It reminded me of something: last time I was here, I met a monk with a similar sort of white dust on his hands. I'd like to speak to him again.'

Suddenly Rufus sat up, his ears pricked.

'What is it?' asked Feng.

'That sound,' said Rufus in surprise. 'I know that sound . . .'

Tip tip tip tip.

Cautiously, Feng and Sienna retreated behind the tree and peered out into the courtyard. A woman wearing a pair of red shoes with sky-high heels was walking across the uneven cobblestones.

Ling.

'The curler-monster! She's here in the temple!' Rufus hissed.

'Let's follow her,' said Sienna.

Feng glanced at her and nodded.

'Have you both lost your minds?' Rufus objected. 'She can see me! That woman and I have history! And her horrible crocodile can't be far behind.'

'Ssh! Just stay close to us,' whispered Sienna, and she hurried after Ling.

Ling didn't notice them amongst the monks and visitors running back and forth among the temple halls, but she was looking around her and seemed to be waiting for someone.

Presently one of the monks went up to her. It was *him*: the plump man with the shiny face and bright blue eyes, in monk's robes once again! Sienna flushed in anger at the sight. Ling greeted him with a fake smile and addressed him as 'Fa Yi'.

The two walked across the yard towards where the three friends were standing. Sienna and Feng glanced at each other in terror, and quickly joined a group of European tourists snapping pictures on their phones, backs turned to Ling and the monk. The pair passed by without a glance. After a few seconds, Sienna and Feng followed, Rufus trotting along at their feet. They didn't even need to stay within view, but hurried after the clacking of Ling's shoes.

They reached a quieter part of the temple. Ling and Fa Yi disappeared behind a wooden door. They heard the sound of a lock turning. Rufus pressed himself up against the door, trying to hear what was being said within. He shook his head in frustration.

'Most annoying,' said Rufus. 'I can't make out a word.'

But Sienna's attention had been caught else-where. Her eyes followed the long hallway to the right of the wooden door, at whose end was another door, a sprinkling of white dust on the handle.

'Come on,' she said, hurrying along the

corridor. She pushed the wooden door open cautiously, her heart pounding. To her disappointment the small, square room was completely empty apart from a few balls of dust on the stone floor and a pile of empty wooden crates. *But that dust on the handle . . . there must be something here*, she thought, scanning the room a second time.

'What now?' asked Feng.

Rufus slipped in behind the others, snuffling at the floor. 'There's . . . something . . . here,' he managed, in between sniffs. He put his paw on the stone floor. 'Feel it.'

Feng bent down and carefully pressed his palm against the floor. 'You're right,' he said finally. 'This part here feels warm.' Sienna tried it too.

Rufus began to sniff the ground again. 'Smells of wood, not stone.'

'Wooden . . . like a door?' said Sienna. 'If only we could find the handle.'

Feng explored the area with his hand. Suddenly he said, 'I've got it!' and a subtle click revealed a square hole in the flagstones.

'I don't like it here at all,' muttered Rufus, while Sienna and Feng pulled up the hatch.

'What are they trying to hide down there?'

Stale, warm air rushed out of the square hole in the floor. At first all they saw was a staircase leading down into darkness, a flicker of light at the bottom.

'You first,' said Rufus.

Together, Sienna and Feng began to go down the steps. When they had reached the bottom they stood there for a while, speechless.

Rufus broke the silence. 'Where are we?'

They were standing in a large chamber. In the centre was a massive levelled block of stone, with tools lying on it. A fluorescent strip light hung overhead. Beside the stone block stood an easel, below which were several colour palettes. Wooden shelves were mounted along the sides of the room, stacked up to the ceiling with works of art. Pictures, statues, jewellery and porcelain were piled high on each shelf.

There was a shuffling noise, and after a brief flicker the room was illuminated in a blaze of neon lighting. 'Who are you?' said a quavering voice.

Sienna spun round. There stood a bowed but broad-shouldered old monk, who looked to be over a hundred years old. Sienna recognized him from his bald head, white eyebrows and the kindness on his face, visible even when he did not smile. It was Sun.

'It's me. Sienna,' she said, her voice a little shaky too. 'We met the other day. This is my friend, Feng.'

'What are you doing down here, children?' the monk asked.

'We're here for the Moon Festival,' said Feng, when Sienna couldn't think up a good excuse. 'We – er – found our way down here by chance.'

The monk looked wary. 'In all these years no one has ever strayed into my workshop by chance. Though I admit it is nice to see someone other than my master,' he sighed, smiling sadly. 'I have lived down here for a long time, entertained only by my work, venturing up to the temple only rarely. There is always so much work to do, you see, so much . . . And now not one, not two, but *three* visitors.' At that the old man bowed to Rufus. The little spaniel growled quietly and Sienna's eyes widened in surprise.

'May we look around?' she said, breaking an awkward silence.

'Be my guest,' smiled the old monk. He returned to an easel set up at the rear of the room, sketching the contours of a landscape in charcoal.

Sienna, Feng and Rufus gazed at the collection with curiosity. Feng picked up several calligraphies while Sienna explored a shelf of pottery and Rufus browsed one bottom shelf after another. Suddenly he exclaimed loudly: 'What's this!' and held out a necklace in his mouth. Sienna took it from him and gasped. It was her grandmother's necklace!

The old monk sighed and set down his charcoal as he saw them looking at the piece. 'Not my best work. Look – it's my third attempt, and still not perfect.' He pulled several more necklaces from the shelf, which all looked identical to the untrained eye. 'Art from distant lands is not my strongest suit,' said Sun. 'I did tell Fa Yi that, but he insisted that I try. He said it was for a new project. And I always like to be of use to him.'

'How can this be? It's impossible!' Rufus was gazing at each identical necklace in amazement. 'This necklace belongs to Sienna's mother – or at least, the original did!'

The old man shook his head, confused.

Rufus turned to Sienna. 'The curler-monster was stealing your mother's jewellery and re-placing it with copies, remember?' Rufus growled, let out an angry bark. 'This man is creating the forgeries!'

The old monk was shocked. 'Fa Yi has always assured me that it was all in honour of the goddess. That she would reward me if I did my work well. Now you tell me he was using my work for criminal activity – for profit!' His eyes filled with tears. 'How stupid I was. I should have guessed.'

Feng looked at the monk searchingly. 'Maybe you can help us with something.'

'Of course. What is it?' said Sun, turning towards him, his face composed.

Feng reached into his pocket and pulled out a dirty bundle of cloth. Unwrapping the statue, he passed it to the monk.

Sun smiled. 'Aha, this one is only *almost* perfect, sadly. I created a perfect statue for my master only yesterday. It's flawless. It took a long time to reach that result. Look!' The ancient monk carefully pulled down a box from the shelf and placed it on the floor. Inside the box were many more identical statues, wrapped in cloth.

Rufus's eyes widened. 'I don't believe it. There are more than twenty of the things, and they all look the same.'

Sienna knelt down on the floor by the statues. Carefully she picked up one after another. 'I can't spot any flaws.' She turned to the monk.

'No, not at first sight,' said the monk, a glimmer of pride in his bright, brown eyes. 'You have to look very closely. But none of the statues is perfect – except the last one. My master has already taken it to a special place. It will be shown tonight as part of our Moon Festival cele-brations. I'm rarely allowed away from this workshop, but even I can feel the full moon rising.' He beamed at Sienna and Feng proudly.

'What is going to happen with the statue, and how is it connected to the full moon?' Sienna whispered hoarsely.

'Aah, there will be the most tremendous spectacle.' The monk's face lit up as he leant closer to Sienna, holding one of the imperfect statues. Feng stepped closer to watch. 'This white stone is very rare and special – it's as porous as plaster or ceramic.'

'You mean . . . it soaks up water?' asked Sienna, remembering how the stone in the mine had felt damp against her fingers.

'That's right, child. A soft glaze on the finish of the statue creates a layer on the outside that water cannot penetrate. But here' – he pointed to the statue's delicately carved eyes – 'here I've left the glaze off. Before the ceremony tonight, Fa Yi will fill the cavity of the statue with oil – through here, see?'

Sienna and Feng peered closely at a minuscule dent in the head of the figurine.

'This was the most difficult part to get right! But in the latest statue, the opening is invisible. It takes a few minutes for the oil to penetrate the eyes – enough time for the opening speech, perhaps. But then—'

'The statue will cry,' breathed Feng.

'Yes. On the night of the Moon Festival, when the moon is full, the statue will begin to weep. Just like the goddess Guanyin. The spectacle will draw more to follow her way, to take the path of mercy. To bring more peace into this world.' He sighed. 'I only wish I could leave my work and see it myself, but I must meet my vow to serve the goddess the best way I can, to continue my work down here, even tonight.'

Feng, Sienna and Rufus stared at each other, stunned.

Sienna didn't understand at first. She stared again at the statues in the box. What were Ling and Fa Yi trying to achieve by forging this statue, over and over, until it was perfect enough to fool an expert? Forging a statue that would weep?

Gradually she pieced it together. 'Fa Yi tricked my mother into thinking she'd discovered something priceless, but she figured out it was forged. That must be why they've imprisoned her!' She clenched her fists as realization gripped her, but Feng finished her thought.

'That's why they're making her write a book to make it seem like the real thing!' he said.

'And that,' said Rufus darkly, 'is why they need to get rid of her as soon as it's done.'

If she's still alive, Mum's in more danger than ever, Sienna realized. She would've felt terrified if she weren't quite so angry.

'I'm so sorry you have been made to work

down here,' she said softly to the monk, angry too at the labour he'd been forced into by Fa Yi. 'We will make sure those who have deceived you so badly are punished for their cruelty.'

At that moment there was a horrible rumbling sound from above. The group looked up at the hatch in the ceiling, which opened as quick as lightning. With a mighty leap a terrible animal jumped down into the workshop and Sienna started backwards, her hands instinctively balled into fists. She hadn't seen it up close last time, and she wished she didn't have to now.

It was huge – much taller than her dad. On its greenish, bulky, half-human body, an ugly head like a crocodile's leered from a thick scaled neck. Crocodile claws sharp as talons glinted from the ends of muscular arms.

'What's that?!' shouted Feng. This was, of course, the first time he had been able to see the creature!

'Ling's monster,' Sienna replied. She sounded much calmer than she felt.

'Oh, not you again,' said Rufus with a groan.

'Get back!' Sienna called to Sun. The old monk hurried to the far end of the room and hid in a small alcove. The crocodile monster bellowed and rushed at Sienna and Feng, saliva dripping from its mouth.

As before, Rufus leapt forwards protectively, a growl building in the back of his throat. The monster hesitated and Rufus snapped at his ankle bravely, but a savage kick sent him hurtling into the shelves in a ball of black fur.

'Rufus!' shouted Sienna, rushing to his side.

The monster cried out, enraged by the dog's attack.

Now Feng stood in front of Sienna and Rufus, his fists clenched. 'Go away!' he shouted. 'Leave us alone!'

The crocodile monster drew back its huge clawed hand, aiming for a punch. Suddenly a huge bang sounded from above, hurried foot-steps thumped on the stairs and a familiar roar filled the air as Xiaolong shot into the workshop and breathed a huge fireball at the monster. Sienna marvelled at how strong and brave the little dragon had become already, with Feng's love and faith!

The crocodile howled in agony, shaking its head in pain.

'Xiaolong!' cried Feng joyfully, as the dragon looped over his head.

An old man burst into the room next, breathless.

'And Zou!' said Sienna, a rush of courage straightening her shoulders.

The monster, recovered from the dragon's attack, reached out for Xiaolong with its hooked claws. Desperate to protect his friend, Feng grabbed a chisel from the bench and ran towards the crocodile monster, jabbing the crude weapon towards its stomach. The beast swatted him away effortlessly and he tumbled into the nearby worktop, priceless treasures crashing to the floor. Xiaolong zoomed to his side while Sienna jumped backwards as a porcelain jug smashed at her feet.

The monster approached Feng, its yellow eyes flashing, huge teeth glinting in the dim light as it loomed over Sienna's friend. She shouted and rushed towards its back, adrenaline pushing through her terror. She had to save Feng!

'Enough!' said Zou. The sharp tone of his voice stopped Sienna in her tracks and the croc-odile spun around. The doctor walked towards the monster. He seemed suddenly younger, taller and stronger.

The huge crocodile opened its awful mouth and snapped at Zou's head, but the old man jumped impossibly high in the air and kicked out at the monster with all his strength. The monster fell to the ground, smacking its skull on the stone wall. It lay very still, but Sienna could tell it was still breathing.

Feng – now recovered – rushed again at the monster on the ground with the chisel in his hand. 'Stop!' cried Zou, restraining the boy with his arm. 'We're not going to kill it. The best way to ensure we never see this monster again is to make sure its mistress, Ling, comes to justice. It is she who has made him become so despicable and violent.'

Rufus heaved himself upright, grumbling. 'Urgh,' he managed, shaking his black coat. 'Fighting crocodiles is hard work!'

Sienna laughed and ran her fingers through his fur. 'I'm glad you're all right, Rufus.'

Xiaolong settled on Feng's shoulder, stretching his broadening wings.

'What happened?' said Feng to his invisible

friend. 'Where's Gege? Did you and Minka find him and Sienna's mother?' But the little dragon's only reply was a shower of yellow sparks.

Sun emerged from his hiding place in the small alcove. 'I'm going to go up to the temple now,' said the old monk. He was visibly confused and shaken, but his eyes were bright with excitement. 'I feel free at last and full of bravery – I can't wait to taste the fresh air and feel the wind against my skin tonight. To witness the festival in honour of Guanyin. Thank you all.'

'You can witness the great spectacle you have helped to create too,' said Zou, picking up Bai tuzi, who'd been hiding in his pocket. 'It's going to be a memorable evening for the temple.'

观音

16 Guanyin

As Sienna and her friends returned to the crowds upstairs, Hong Yi – the young monk who Sienna had spoken to at the temple just the day before – appeared before them. He bowed to Sienna, glancing quizzically at her injured head.

Although Sienna's heart thumped, she did her best to appear calm. 'Good evening, Hong Yi. This is my friend Feng.'

Hong Yi bowed to Feng, though he gave him a

slightly strange look. Feng was covered in dust from the mine, and he looked nervous, brushing his dark hair in front of his face and folding his arms across his grubby T-shirt. 'I'm very glad that you have both come along this evening,' said Hong Yi, pushing his glasses up his nose. 'This is the occasion for which the honourable Kate worked so hard, and I promise you that we are all going to experience something wonderful. Please follow me.'

They followed the monk to the courtyard. Tonight, the space was filled with plastic chairs set out in rows, circling around the brightly decorated well at its centre. Paper lanterns threw a warm yellow glow through the temple arches, lighting the faces of the gathering audience.

But the lamplight was nothing compared to the full moon. Sienna's eyes were drawn to the sky. Now at its peak, the moon was so large and clear that she could see the grey circles of mountains and craters on its surface. Its silvery light was bright enough to cast shadows. It was the most beautiful moon she had ever seen.

'It's amazing,' said Feng, his eyes fixed on the sky.

'It is,' Sienna whispered, as they hurried after Hong Yi. 'But we should watch out for Ling and Fa Yi. They're about to reveal their fake statue – we can't let them get away with it.' She combed the crowd, suddenly anxious, but she couldn't see Ling anywhere among their upturned faces. Nor could she see Minka, or her mum, or even Zou. Where had *he* disappeared to?

'Hurry up,' grumbled Rufus. 'I need to lie down. Defeating that crocodile monster was exhausting.'

Sienna couldn't suppress a giggle.

Hong Yi led them to the first row, right at the front of the hall, where several seats had been reserved. Sienna could feel people's eyes upon them as they sat down and she realized they must look a strange sight amongst the crowd wearing their finery: a blonde girl with a head injury wearing odd clothes, and a boy covered in dust. Rufus flopped on her lap with a dramatic sigh.

The young monk bent down to speak to Sienna. 'All the important people of Pingding-shan are gathered here this evening. Even the mayor is here. Your mother has achieved great things for us – please accept my thanks on her behalf.'

'Um, OK. Thanks,' said Sienna, smiling nervously. *But I wish I didn't have to*, she thought, a knot of worry tightening in her stomach. *Where is she? Is she OK?*

'I have to go – the fireworks are about to begin,' continued Hong Yi. 'The abbot is leading us in a procession after the display. I hope you enjoy this very special evening.' He bowed and walked away.

Just then Sienna heard a bell tinkle and Minka leapt up on to her lap, right next to Rufus, who grumbled under his breath and shuffled aside. 'Don't say anything right now, Sienna,' the cat ordered, before Sienna could react. 'We don't want to draw attention to ourselves.'

Feng glanced across at Minka, smiling a silent 'hello'.

Sienna kept quite still, although she wanted to hug the cat and ask her where her mum was.

The fireworks started, bright trails of light shooting high into the sky and exploding in showers of red, green and gold like enormous weeping willows. Wheels of pink squealed across the surface of the moon. Xiaolong was flying excited loop-de-loops over Feng's head – he loved it. The crowd did too, cheering and gasping, clapping wildly at every bang.

'What's happening with Mum? Did you find her?' Sienna whispered to Minka under the tumult. Feng leant in close to listen.

'All's well with her,' replied Minka. 'The little dragon helped me rescue her and your friend's brother from the cave. They're here, waiting for the right moment.'

Sienna's heart was so full of excitement and happiness that she felt it might burst! She wanted to ask more questions but the fireworks had ended and a gong struck loudly, reverberating through the air. Silence descended upon the crowd. A great many monks now walked in pairs through the temple courtyard, with one man – the abbot, Sienna realized – at their head.

The abbot. Sienna's breath caught in her throat. *It was Fa Yi.* She nudged Feng in the ribs. 'It's *him*,' she whispered. 'He was the one with the knife.'

'It'll be all right,' Feng replied, squeezing her

arm, but Sienna wished she could be so sure.

She tried to make out the other monks' faces, but they were too far away. Then the last monk caught her eye. He was walking alone and his gait looked familiar to Sienna. Was that Zou, by any chance?

Sure enough, Bai tuzi's sparkly dust fell from the monk's right shoulder on to the floor. Sienna felt a little better, knowing they were nearby.

The monks now positioned themselves in the centre of the courtyard, surrounding the holy well. Hong Yi stood alongside the abbot. 'In the name of our abbot and all the monks of this monastery I would like to welcome you all cordially to the Fragrant Mountain Temple. At tonight's Moon Festival I have the immeasurable honour of celebrating with you a discovery which will make this temple one of the most celebrated places in China, and indeed one of the most celebrated places in the Buddhist world. We owe this discovery to a young woman, Dr Kate Farringdon, who sadly disappeared a few months ago without a trace. Whilst undertaking research in our temple, Dr Farringdon made a great discovery. This evening we will present this discovery to the world.'

Fa Yi bent down and carefully lifted up a box. Placing it on a small table in front of him, he took out an object wrapped in pieces of white cloth, and carefully removed the covering.

The perfect statue. It really did look magical in the moonlight and the audience gasped, then watched the abbot with awe. The moon shone brightly down upon everyone, giving their faces a ghostly pallor.

Hong Yi went to the abbot's side. 'This statue is a depiction of Guanyin. As everyone knows, this holy well is the very place where Guanyin wept tears of mercy for her father under the full moon, curing him at the cost of her own life and securing her place in the pantheon of the gods. This temple was first built in her honour. Sadly, academics have claimed that the story of the princess that turned into a goddess is relatively modern, and therefore its authenticity has been doubted . . .' He paused, a small smile playing at his lips, as if he could barely contain his excitement. 'But this statue – discovered in the grounds of the temple itself – is very old. It tells us that the goddess must have been known to people since ancient times. After extensive research, we have discovered that the statue was produced around the time of the princess herself.' He smiled broadly. 'The legend is true.'

The crowd murmured excitedly and began to stand up, trying to get a better look at the statue.

'How can I prove this, my friends?' Hong Yi continued. 'It is not I who have done so, but the famous art historian, Dr Farringdon. She discovered the statue in our temple, and her notes leave no room for any doubt as to the authenticity of this work of art. This' – Hong Yi lifted a stack of papers in the air – 'this book was written by Dr Farringdon shortly before her disappearance.'

Sienna wanted to stand up and rip the papers out of Hong Yi's hand. She felt a rush of pure anger. Was the monk in league with Ling and Fa Yi? How else could Hong Yi have come by the book Mum had written while she was being held prisoner? And he had pretended to be kind to her!

'This discovery,' Hong Yi now cried loudly, 'will make our temple the centre for worship of the goddess!' He raised both his hands and the audience applauded enthusiastically.

Suddenly Fa Yi let out a cry of amazement and fell to his knees. 'She is crying!' exclaimed the abbot loudly. 'The statue is weeping!'

Other monks crowded around, gasping as they too watched the tears trickling from Guanyin's eyes. Feng stood up and Sienna followed suit, Rufus and Minka tumbling from her lap with a growl and a screech. From her seat at the front, she too could see the spectacle and Sienna had to admit that the sight of the statue weeping in the mysterious light of the full moon was captivating and haunting.

But she knew it was a lie!

An audience member dashed forward from nearby. 'It's true!' the man exclaimed. 'Guanyin weeps – just as she wept for her father in the ancient tale. It's a miracle!'

Chaos suddenly reigned. Even if she'd wanted to, Sienna couldn't have got anyone's attention to tell them the truth. Everyone was calling out at the same time and many people pulled out phones and cameras and tried to photograph the monks with the statue. Then they began to bow down in reverence, and some fell to their knees.

Fa Yi held the statue above his head in his clasped hand, and cried, 'On the night of the Moon Festival, Guanyin grieves for the people. She is with us. She *feels* all our pain!' His bright blue eyes appeared to glow. Sienna hated to admit it, but the performance was very convincing – he was getting away with it!

Suddenly there was a loud crash. It was coming from the tree at the side of the courtyard, from which several crows now took to the air, cawing loudly.

The people all looked at the tree as suddenly, in rapid succession, small white packages began to fall from it.

'I think you'll want to see what's in those packages!' chuckled Rufus.

Sienna and Feng ran towards the tree. Looking up into the branches she saw Bai tuzi perched on a branch. He winked at her. Sienna picked up a few of the packages and started unwinding the white cloth. In her hands she held the same statue Hong Yi was displaying on the stage in front of her. And tears ran down the face of her statue too. She knew at once that these statues were the ones from Sun's workshop, each one slightly imperfect. Zou must've filled each one with oil to prove the miracle had been faked – that's where he'd disappeared to after leaving the workshop!

Hurriedly she and Feng started unwrapping the rest of the packages. The audience stared in disbelief as, one after the other, the crying statues were exposed to the moonlight. Rufus, Minka and Xiaolong sat nearby.

Sienna collected all the statues she could carry and, with Feng's help, carried them along the pathway through the crowd opened up by the curious spectators. She stopped in front of the monks and laid the pile of statues at their feet. 'I think you'll want to see these,' she said, her voice loud and clear.

The monks stared in bewilderment at the heap of identical statues, below which a puddle of tears was slowly forming. Fa Yi's face paled, his skin now as white as the statues' stone, his hands trembling. His blue eyes darted around the courtyard.

Hong Yi bent down and picked up one of the goddesses from the ground, holding it alongside the statue in his hand to compare the two.

'What's going on here? Where have these come from? Abbot?' His lip was trembling. 'You promised it was real!'

'This stupid girl is trying to deceive us all, to cheapen this incredible miracle and disrespect the goddess!' said Fa Yi, his voice shaking. 'Remove her! That's an order!'

But nobody moved.

'It's over, Fa Yi,' said Sienna firmly.

Rufus was on one side of her, Minka on the other. Feng and Xiaolong stood nearby while Zou hovered at the back of the huddle of monks, smiling at Sienna. As the old monk Sun stepped forward from behind Zou, the monks and the audience stared at their leader in disbelief and Sienna knew she had won.

The abbot returned her stare, his eyes full of hatred. Then he broke away and made a dash, pushing past the crowd towards the exit.

'Stop him!' screamed Sienna. 'Someone stop him!'

在一起

17 Zai yiqi - Together

Spurred into action at the fear in Sienna's voice, a man from the crowd stuck out his leg to trip up the monk, sending Fa Yi sprawling on the ground. Another audience member wrestled him to his feet and dragged him to the front. The crowd watched the whole spectacle, mesmerized.

'But I don't understand,' stammered Hong Yi. 'The statue *must* be genuine. Your mother knew it. Your mother was the one who found it!'

'Yes, the way you planned it all along,' said a voice from somewhere amidst the group of monks.

The men moved aside and the crowd gasped as a tall blonde woman walked up to Hong Yi. It was Sienna's mum! Minka dashed to her side, rubbed her head against Kate's shins, and Sienna saw her mum's eyes flicker to the ground, a small smile on her lips.

Kate's green eyes were flashing in her pale face, and her hair shone brightly in the light of the moon. Sienna couldn't move – she couldn't breathe! Tears filled her eyes. Silently, Feng clasped her hand.

'Fa Yi has tricked us all. I was stupid enough to believe him that this statue was genuine. And you, Hong Yi, are blinded by your own obsession. Your obsession with making the temple famous.'

'Mrs Kate!' whispered Hong Yi, turning pale. 'How is this possible? Where have you been all this time?'

Kate turned to the crowd. 'I was captured and taken prisoner, Hong Yi. Along with my friend, Gege. They forced me to finish writing the book about the temple. They threatened to do something to my daughter if I didn't obey them. Finally they trapped us in a mine and were going to leave us to die,' said Sienna's mother, her strong voice fading.

Sienna could wait no longer. She pushed her way through the crowd and ran into her mother's arms. The two of them stood silently, locked together, tears running down both their faces. The spectators had fallen completely silent.

A man got up from his seat and walked to the front. 'In my capacity as police chief of Pingdingshan I am ordering an investigation into these events. We will take the monk Fa Yi into custody for questioning.'

Fa Yi shrieked angrily and pointed wildly at the back of the crowd. 'It's her you want! Not me, *her*! It was all her idea!'

Kate and Sienna turned to see Ling trying to sneak out of the temple courtyard, her high heels noisily marking her exit. As she reached the door a young man stepped in front of her, blocking her way.

'That's Gege!' Feng shouted to Sienna, his face lighting up in a huge smile at the sight of his brother.

Ling desperately tried to push Gege aside, but he was too strong. The police chief sent two officers to drag her up to the front of the crowd and Gege and Feng hugged each other tightly, as if they never wanted to let go again.

'Little brother, forgive me. I never meant to leave you alone,' Sienna heard Gege murmur under his breath. Xiaolong flapped his wings happily overhead.

Ling came face to face with both Sienna and Kate.

'You're pathetic,' hissed Kate. 'I've heard all about your cruel treatment of my daughter. You will never be allowed to hurt anyone again.'

Sienna smiled brightly at Ling. She'd carried such feelings of hatred for Ling but now, her mum's arm around her shoulders, she felt nothing but pity for this awful woman. 'I feel sorry for you,' she whispered. 'We have each other, but you only have that horrible monster!'

Ling shrieked furiously and pushed towards Sienna, but another pair of hands held her back. Sienna's dad! As the police officers took the criminals away he embraced his wife and daughter, silent sobs wracking his body.

None of those present noticed as Zou left and headed away from the temple. He picked up Bai tuzi and stroked his fur carefully. Glitter dust sparkled in the moonlight as it fell to the ground.

'My dear friend, what a great adventure this has been. But now it's time for us to go.' He smiled. 'I thought we'd keep this one' – he pulled a statue out of his monk's habit – 'as a souvenir.'

The perfect forgery lay in his hand, gleaming white in the light of the moon.

Later that night, Sienna, Feng, Gege, Kate, Dad and the invisible friends all sat in Dad's hotel room. Everyone was exhausted and barely able to speak, a mixture of joy and disbelief robbing them of language. The adults sat on the armchairs in the room, while Sienna and Feng lay on the king-size bed. Rufus and Minka too had made themselves comfortable on the soft cushions. The little dragon was asleep beside Feng.

Sienna looked at her parents contentedly. At the temple Dad had taken Mum in his arms for a long time, as though he never wanted to let her go. Mum had pulled Sienna towards them and the three of them had embraced.

'I feel awful,' muttered Sienna's dad. 'I didn't believe that you could still be alive, I should have done more to find you—'

'Stop that,' said Mum firmly. 'The only one to blame here is Ling, and that crooked abbot Fa Yi. Although it has to be said that Fa Yi has a great talent for forgery.'

'Fa Yi didn't forge the statues and the jewellery himself, though,' Sienna pointed out. She explained about the poor old monk who had been misled by him, who had worked so hard for him in the cellar.

Mum shook her head in disbelief. 'I'm sure the monks will take care of him, but we'll check tomorrow that he is all right.'

'Was Hong Yi as guilty as Fa Yi and Ling?' asked Sienna. She felt a bit bad for the young monk. Surely he had only wanted to do what he thought was best for the temple?

Sienna's mother thought about it for a moment. 'He desperately wanted the temple to be famous. When Hong Yi found out that a statue existed which could help the temple attain greater fame, he didn't ask too many questions. Sometimes we believe what we want to believe – I was guilty of that too,' she said. 'The abbot knew that my expertise would draw a lot of attention to the statue. He thought it would be better if I "discovered" the statue myself. And it wasn't long before I did.'

Here, Kate smiled at Gege, who looked ashamed.

'At first I didn't spot any of the clues that pointed to a forgery. I *wanted* to believe the statue was genuine. But when I examined the statue more closely, I noticed something wasn't quite right about the eyes – and that's when I realized it was a forgery, specially designed to weep. When I expressed my concerns to Fa Yi, he was very angry. That's when I knew something was wrong. I was on the point of going to the police.'

'But then Ling kidnapped you,' said Sienna. 'With you out of the way the forger had time to produce an even more convincing forgery and you had to write your report stating that the statue was genuine.'

'Exactly,' said Mum, hugging Sienna. 'Ling blackmailed me. For the first few months it was just threats – and I simply used the time to continue writing my book, to take my mind off my situation, though I worried terribly about you, my darling. But then Ling showed me photos of you and Dad in Shanghai. I didn't even know that the two of you were in China. I was so frightened you'd be in danger, so I had to do as they said. Write what they wanted.'

'Sienna.' Dad sat down next to her on the bed, looking concerned. 'How on earth did you and Feng discover that Mum and Gege were down at the mines? And how did you manage to get to the temple on your own? Someone must have helped you, surely?'

'Careful what you say, my little moon princess. Best not mention the white sparkly hare or the little fire-breather.' Rufus could hardly contain his laughter.

'Or that you cycled through the night on an old bike, led by a magical white cat,' purred Minka.

Sienna shot them a furious glance! Mum caught her eye and winked. 'Feng knew a few people,' said Sienna finally. 'Then we met a man, a doctor. Doctor Zou. He helped us.'

Mum went to Sienna and gave her a kiss on the forehead. 'Now we must get some rest, tomorrow's another day for talking.' She hugged Sienna tightly. 'I've arranged for you two to stay here at the hotel too,' she said, turning to Gege and Feng, giving Gege a hug and handing them a room key.

After the others had left, Sienna lay awake next to her mum. She'd wanted to sleep with her parents tonight. Rufus was snoring quietly at the foot of the bed and Dad was sound asleep on Mum's other side.

'Mum?' whispered Sienna.

'What is it, my darling?' her mother answered.

'Did you see Minka, in the mines?' asked Sienna.

There was a moment of silence. 'Funny you should ask,' said Mum. 'You know, when I was imprisoned and feeling hopeless, I did feel as if she was with me. Sometimes I even heard the bell on her collar. And then, after the explosion in the mine, I dreamt I was a little girl again, with Minka waking me up by pawing me in the face. I woke up and there were clouds of fire and a passage had opened in the wall. I glimpsed her

then, leading me and Gege out into the light –
and the whole time I could hear a little bell
tinkling. Remarkable, isn't it?'

'Why did she go away, when you were
younger?' Sienna asked.

'Probably because I sent her away,' Mum
replied, with a sigh. 'I decided real friends were
more important. And I grew up. Lots of reasons,
really. Sometimes I think some other little girl
needed Minka more than I did – but she came
back for me when it really mattered, didn't she?
Good friends never really disappear, even when
you can't see them any more. Now, time to rest.
Sleep well,' said Mum, and she cuddled up
closely to Sienna.

EPILOGUE
Zhongguo – China, the Middle Kingdom

Sienna looked out of the window at the river.

Dad had rented a new flat. It was comfortable here and she liked the view. China was beginning to feel like home. She was starting at her new school the following week. She smiled: in the past, the thought of new teachers and classmates would have scared her, but this time she wouldn't be alone. Her parents were so grateful to Feng that when they heard about what had happened to him they had decided to help him and Gege.

Dad had found a job for Gege with his employers in Shanghai, and Mum and Dad were also going to pay Feng's school fees. Dad was very happy that Sienna finally had a real friend. He'd have been rather less happy if he had known that Rufus and Xiaolong were the two children's constant companions!

Minka, however, had bid them farewell. 'It's time for me to leave,' she had told them, rubbing up against Sienna's hand one final time. 'Your mother's moved on, and I need to as well.' Her whiskers twitched. 'Besides, I think there's someone else out there who needs me now.'

The morning after the Moon Festival they had all set out together to visit Zou, but the front door was locked up. Dad and Mum had rung the neighbours' doorbells and asked after Zou, but the people just shrugged their shoulders and shook their heads. *No, there's no one living there,* they said.

Eventually Sienna met an old woman on the street. The woman had smiled when Sienna had asked after Zou.

'It sounds as though you met someone who helped you when you were in great need. All one has to do is trust . . .' she said.

Sienna wished she could have said goodbye to Zou and thanked him for everything. But she felt in her heart that he knew how grateful she was to him and the amazing Bai tuzi!

But Gege had a new job, and Feng had a home and was reunited with Gege. He'd be going to school again, and he was Sienna's friend.

Sienna smiled. She even had her mum back, and her dad. And she'd *always* have Rufus, no matter what!

Many thanks to Weixiang Wang:
friend, doctor and walking dictionary.

What's your invisible animal?

Take this quiz to find out!

1. **You forgot to do your homework. How would your invisible friend help you?**

a. He'd write the most amazing piece of homework for you, even though your teacher might wonder if it's really yours.

b. He'd whisper everything you need to know in your ear, so you can quickly write it down in your own words.

c. He would advise you to go to your teacher and tell the truth. It's the right thing to do, even though you might get in trouble.

d. He would give you a big hug and say homework is overrated, anyway.

e. He would draw an amazing picture of a beautiful landscape in your exercise book that has nothing to do with your homework, but makes your teacher cry.

2. You're new in school and feel a bit lonely. What would your invisible friend do?

a. He'd help you run the fastest time ever at sports day. Everyone talks to you to find out how you did it.
b. He'd point out the other kids who feel alone and encourage you to get to know them.
c. He'd give you a push so you stumble into someone, forcing you to start talking.
d. He would be extra kind and reassuring. Everything is fine as long as you have him.
e. He would help you to organise the most amazing party that everyone wants to come to.

3. You're bored. How does your invisible friend change that?

a. He takes you on a fun, dizzying rollercoaster ride.
b. He sneaks you all your favourite treats and chats to you until you cheer up.
c. You go for a ride on his back through a wild, dangerous forest with the most amazing trees, flowers and animals.
d. He tells you stories of faraway places, so exciting and vivid that it almost feels as if you were there.
e. He takes you to a party to meet lots of new friends and their amazing invisible animals.

4. **If you had to choose a special power for your invisible animal, which would you pick?**

a. You'd love to be able to fly – you'd go all over the world together.
b. The power to understand people's true meanings and feelings would be really useful.
c. A strong and fierce companion would be best, protecting you from other invisible friends and teaching you how to fight.
d. Most of all, you'd like an invisible friend who has the power to sniff out the truth and who is absolutely trustworthy.
e. You'd love a friend with energy, grace and beauty – everyone who sees him will envy you!

5. **Your (visible!) friend isn't speaking to you, but you're not sure why. You ask your invisible friend for advice. What would he say?**

a. 'Don't worry – she'll tell you what's up, or she won't. You just have to be there for her.'
b. 'You should talk to her, find out why she's so quiet. There might be something wrong.'
c. 'It's silly for her to ignore you like this! Ignore her right back.'
d. 'I'm worried. Perhaps we can bake a cake to cheer her up.'
e. 'Who cares? It's not worth the effort. You've got loads of other friends, anyway!'

6. You find £20 on the street. What would your invisible friend tell you to do?

a. He'd tell you you're lucky – finders keepers! Enjoy it.
b. He'd wonder who might have dropped the money and why. Maybe it was important. You should probably ask at the local shop.
c. That money belongs to someone else: it would be wrong for you to take it. Your invisible friend would insist you hand it in to the police.
d. He's not sure what's right, but he won't tell anyone if you keep it ... you probably deserve to buy yourself something nice.
e. Perfect! He'd suggest you treat your best friend to a cinema trip.

What were your answers?

Mostly a: Your invisible friend is a dragon

The dragon is probably the most popular animal in Chinese mythology. He is a symbol of luck and fortune and one of the twelve zodiac signs. Many Chinese people want their child to be born in the year of the dragon. Dragons are supposed to be born leaders. They are idealists and perfectionists and always proud and generous.

Mostly b: Your invisible friend is a rabbit

The most famous rabbit in Chinese mythology is the Jade or Moon Rabbit. It can make medicine and is a symbol for longevity. Children born under the sign of the rabbit are supposed to be sweet and sensitive. The rabbit is an excellent and very thoughtful friend. He understands you like no one else.

Mostly c: Your invisible friend is a tiger

In Chinese mythology the tiger is brave and fearless and protects good people from evil spirits. If a child is born in the year of the tiger, they are competitive, generous and can be real daredevils. The tiger knows what's right or wrong and will fight for the good cause, whatever it takes. He loves adventures.

Mostly d: Your invisible friend is a dog

In the Chinese zodiac, people born under the sign of the dog are seen as loyal and kind. They are warm-hearted and considerate. A dog will never leave his friends alone and can be trusted with all secrets. He is also very honest and will tell you the truth no matter what.

Mostly e: Your invisible friend is a horse

Horses stand for power and virtue. When someone is born under the sign of the horse, they are supposed to be active and energetic. They love being in a crowd and always have a lot of friends. Most of all the horse likes to see and be seen.